A
MURDER IN
GURGAON

A
MURDER IN
GURGAON

Manish Dubey

Srishti
PUBLISHERS & DISTRIBUTORS

Srishti Publishers & Distributors
Registered Office: N-16, C.R. Park
New Delhi – 110 019
Corporate Office: 212A, Peacock Lane
Shahpur Jat, New Delhi – 110 049
editorial@srishtipublishers.com

First published by
Srishti Publishers & Distributors in 2016

To Bharti,
for believing and understanding.

Acknowledgments

Sammar and Nandini, for lighting up my life, for making every day worth looking forward to. Without you, there is no point to this. Or anything else.

Ma and Papa, for always being there, for bearing with my moods, respecting my choices, shooing my worries. I fly because of you and know that I can never repay your debt.

Nani and Nanaji, for listening and indulgence. Sometimes it's all a kid needs. If you were around, I know you would've been the proudest.

Mausi, Mausaji and Mummy, for always placing my convenience above their own, for always being there and never letting the boat rock. I am guilty of not recognizing your sacrifices enough.

Dipti Mukherjee, Gora Chand Mukherjee, Katy Narielwalla, Krishna Bhattacharya, M. Narang, Philip Chalil and Victor Lazarus, teachers who offered affection and encouragement beyond duty's call. Things would've turned out very different without you.

Andy Mukherjee, Bharat Solanky, Sanjay Sangal and Somnath Sen, friends who read the first draft and encouraged me to push ahead. Your generous words, gentlemen, came back to me whenever I felt like giving up. And Ragini Bajaj-Choudhary who didn't need to read the first draft to predict this would see the light of day.

Team Srishti, for patiently seeing this through.

Chintu, I miss you.

Part - I

I think it is all a matter of love; the more you love a memory, the stronger and stranger it becomes.

—Vladimir Nabokov

More than Leena's birthday or their wedding anniversary, it was on days he was called to school to see Sister Flavian that Parikshit Puri missed his long dead wife the most. He entered the nun's odorless, trophy-lined chamber that drizzly morning, prepared to apologize for his daughter's latest shenanigan. Behind her large, cowl-framed head, Jesus bled. Arrayed by the window were the six famous canes.

ॐ

I'll be frank with you, Mr Puri. Leena shows no sign of mending her ways.

All I can say then is that your words haven't had the desired effect. What happened the day before is not something I recall in all my years at Holy Cross Convent.

A faculty member found her exchanging letters with a boy from the school next door. This was during lunch recess. You can see the letters yourself. There are words here I cannot bring myself to speak aloud.

Her attitude despite being caught red-handed has been no less disturbing. We see no trace of shame or remorse.

The matter was serious enough to be placed before the School Governing Council. I've been asked to convey the Council's decision to you.

The Council believes a change in schooling environment would be good for Leena.

Yes. That's what is being suggested.

It's not just about what happened the day before. Though that alone, mind you, would invite the strictest action in any self-respecting school. You are well aware of the past complaints. Our most experienced teachers are at their wits' end. Co-parents say she's an unhealthy influence on their wards. Those points were considered too.

I'm afraid you won't find the Council flexible in this matter. Members feel there have been too many leniencies already. We are all, honestly speaking, tired.

Please, Mr Puri, please. You don't have to apologize on her behalf. Leena is thirteen now. A young lady. Old enough to know right and wrong, be accountable for her actions.

I understand. Any other person in your position would feel the same. However, may I urge you to pause and reflect carefully on the entire situation? At Holy Cross Convent, your daughter has, unfortunately, come to be viewed as a rebel, a problem child. Even if she were to make amends now, everyone – her peers, her teachers, your co-parents – will continue to look at her differently. She'll carry the label for all her years here. At some point, it is bound to scar her mentally. I'm sure that's not something you want. On the other hand, she will have the benefit of a clean slate in another school.

We understand raising a girl alone isn't easy for a father, Mr Puri. You have all our sympathies. But you will appreciate we are running an educational institution here, an institution trusted by families for over fifty years to inculcate the right values in their girls. Any action that compromises our values, any development that shakes parents' faith in us, is naturally unwelcome from the institution's perspective.

I am sorry. There's absolutely no scope for reconsideration. The Council's decision was unanimous.

It would be in everyone's best interest if the shift happens at the earliest.

End of session then? That would be sufficient time?

End of session is the best I can do from my side.

Of course, you will get a proper school-leaving certificate. There should be no worry on that account. The idea isn't to tar the child for life, but to give her a fair chance for redemption. In a setting that might be more suitable to her temperament.

I want you to know this conversation gives me no pleasure at all. However, we have had Leena's long-term interests in mind while making the decision, and I am confident that its benefits will be on display in time. There's no doubt in any of our minds that she's a bright girl.

ॐ

En route home, Parikshit Puri thought how much easier life would have been, had Leena inherited his quietude. She was, mostly but not always for good, her mother's daughter.

FEBRUARY 1987

The VIII B girls took turns to read out farewell messages. Mrs Midha wasn't surprised to see Leena uninterested. A horrible thing to admit, but she was relieved, glad almost, to see the Puri girl go.

Mrs Midha had heard of Leena from the previous class teacher, decided to keep an open mind, discovered the girl was trouble in the first week itself. First hand. When she overheard a conversation inside the chemistry lab.

Leena Puri: I'm going to burn my sanitary napkin next time.

Kamna Vohra (amidst eeks from other girls): Why?

Leena Puri: A girl who burns her used sanitary napkin with her own hand becomes barren.

Fiona Andrews: Barren?

Leena Puri: She can never get pregnant.

Laxmi Chawla: So?

Leena Puri: So she can have all the fun she wants with boys without worrying about getting a baby in her tummy, stupid.

The words were spoken with authority, enough authority to make Mrs Midha wonder if she had missed a convenient, foolproof contraception option herself. She didn't report the matter to Sister Flavian, didn't know how to.

Mrs Midha: Ready now, Bindia? You are the last one left. Leena is not coming to school from tomorrow.

Bindia Khosla is sobbing.

Leena Puri (waving a piece of paper): She's written this poem for me, Mrs Midha. I can read it out.

Mrs Midha (ignoring Leena): Let's hear from you, Bindia. Leena's your best friend, isn't it? All of us are waiting to hear what you have to say.

Bindia Khosla continues sobbing.

Mrs Midha (starts off mildly irritated, eases midway): Enough, Bindia, enough. You can write to Leena, meet her when she's in Delhi to visit her grandparents. You'll come down to see them during holidays, won't you, Leena?

Leena Puri (shrugs): I can read her poem out.

Mrs Midha (reluctantly): Fine. Girls, this is from Bindia. Go ahead, Leena.

I am feeling bad
And very, very sad
Because my friend's going away
In just another day
Going to America, she is
It's across seven seas
My loss will be someone's gain
Oh, when will I meet her again?
I hope she writes to me real quick
Otherwise I will be worried sick
I don't know what more to say
All there is to do is pray.

FEBRUARY 2014

[Scene: Inside a flight.]

Awoman and a man are talking softly. The man comes across as flirty; the woman inclined to play along. They smile at each other, lock eyes often.

Announcement: Ladies and gentlemen, as we start our descent, please make sure your seat backs and tray tables are in their full upright position. Make sure your seat belt is securely fastened...

The man (glancing at his watch): SkyLine, on time as usual.

The woman nods in agreement.

The man: It's been great talking to you.

The woman: Good to hear that.

The man: The pleasure isn't mutual then?

The woman: I said what I felt.

The man: I don't do this often.

The woman: What?

The man: Strike a conversation with a female co-passenger.

The woman: Is that so?

The man: Not such a personal conversation anyway.

The woman: If you say so.

The man: You find it difficult to believe?

The woman: Going by your lines, yes.

The man: What about my lines?

The woman: Let's just say they seem...umm...tried and tested.

The man: Caught me. And are such conversations usual for you?

The woman: No. Not usual.

The man: Aren't you going to ask why I started off?

The woman: You seem keen to tell.

The man: You keen to hear too?

The woman: Nobody's stopping you.

The man: It may sound corny but it's the eyes.

The woman: That's a first.

The man: What?

The woman: A compliment for my eyes.

The man: Ah. You've been complimented on other things.

The woman: Fair deduction.

The man: What other things? Or do you want me to guess?

The woman: Guess.

The man: Warning. From what I see, it could take time.

The woman: Really? That's...bold.

The man: By the way, I didn't get your name?

The woman: You haven't asked yet.

The man: I am asking now.

The woman: Leena.

The man: Leena?

The woman: Leena Puri.

The man: Mrs Leena Puri?

Leena Puri: Does it matter?

The man: Not to me.

Leena Puri: Guessed as much.

The man: I bet Leena isn't your real name.

Leena Puri: Maybe not. Déjà vu?

The man: You can say that. I am Pratik Kaul.

Leena Puri: Real name, I assume?

Pratik Kaul: Oh, yes. Honesty is the best policy.

Leena Puri: Hard to disagree with a statement so profound.

Pratik Kaul: Pulling my leg, madam?

Leena Puri: You would like that, wouldn't you?

Pratik Kaul: On that note, another question. How do we keep in touch?

Leena Puri: We don't, Mr Kaul. We don't.

Pratik Kaul (makes a sob face): That's unkind.

Leena Puri: A line has to be drawn somewhere.

Pratik Kaul: My bad luck.

Leena Puri: Shall I tell you something?

Pratik Kaul: All ears, madam.

Leena Puri (with a sudden hint of ice): I believe people make their own luck. And a no, Mr Kaul, means no.

[Before Pratik Kaul responds, Leena Puri turns away, starts looking out of the window. He doesn't seem too perturbed by the snub. A smile appears on her lips as she notices him absorbing himself in the in-flight magazine from the corner of her eye.]

Part - II

Friendship is one mind in two bodies.

—Mencius

There are no strangers here; only friends you have never met.

—William Butler Yeats

Leena picked the skirt for her. A fitted geometric pattern A-line skirt that ended above the knee wasn't something Bindia would have tried otherwise. The mirror confirmed, yet again, her best friend's excellent taste. Bindia's makeover, a makeover that even Ashok had noticed, had everything to do with Leena.

The last piece of the ensemble for Sheena Chopra's Christmas party finalized, they proceeded to Aroma. Since Bindia had decided not to moan about her woes, there was, for once, something else to talk about – Leena's plans to launch a reiki healing practice. Bindia was genuinely happy to hear the enthusiasm in Leena's voice.

The parting was unusually sentimental. Bindia tearfully thanked Leena for being there for her, freeing her in so many ways. Leena said that's what friends were for. God, fate, destiny, whatever, separated people, and brought them back together with a purpose. That purpose was not to be questioned or analyzed, but accepted-as-good.

The philosophy bothered Bindia; it meant Leena was slipping again. Not for the first time, she wished Leena would talk, spit out whatever was eating her from within. Something clearly was, but Bindia didn't dare ask. Asking Leena a personal question was the surest way to get her pissed. The Leena she knew would open when she wanted, about what she wanted.

Before getting up, they toasted their friendship with empty cups. They went back a long time. To school. Where they had been the two motherless girls in class.

Motherless girls with pesky grandparents, smothering aunts, and clueless fathers.

ॐ

[141 Killed in Pak School Attack]

Please do not worry, Mrs Sehgal. Jaidev is safe. Everyone is.

[Taliban Justifies Massacre Of Children]

The boys have just finished games hour and returned to their dorm. None of them knows about the incident yet. The housemasters will be speaking to them shortly, over tea.

['Classmates Killed In Front Of Us']

We have arranged a special call slot between 7 to 9 p.m. today and tomorrow. You can speak to Jaidev then. It's best we have a chance to talk to the boys first.

['One Of My Children Still Missing']

The Headmaster has called a Housemasters' meeting later today to review security. Colonel Swamy from the security department will join too. At this point, all I am authorized to share is that no effort or expense will be spared to strengthen our security set-up. You can expect a detailed communication on the whole issue from the Headmaster in the coming days.

[Pak PM: Attack, A National Tragedy]

Luckily, the boys are leaving for the winter break the day after. That gives us time to work on any additional security measures that may be needed. Jaidev, of course, is directly headed for Australia for the schoolboys' cricket tour.

[Pak PM: Children Killed Are Mine]

Yes, between 7 to 9 p.m. today and tomorrow. We are advising all parents to speak calmly. Our anxieties will only raise the boys' fears.

[Pak Army: All Attackers Killed, 900 Rescued]

Once again, please be assured that the boys are in safe hands. May I also request you to inform Mr Sehgal of Jaidev's wellbeing? He would be concerned too.

[Barbaric, Cowardly, Say World Leaders]

You're welcome, Mrs Sehgal. On a separate topic, both of you will be happy to know that Jaidev is well prepared for the Australian tour and very much looking forward to it.

॰ৎ

Leena made a brief, decidedly odd call around 8.15 p.m. Had a migrainous Bindia not been occupied with getting through to Jai over the uninterruptedly busy line to Blue Mountain International (Boys), she would have tried to find more.

Waking up to pee around 10.30 p.m., Bindia tried Leena's number. It was switched off. She didn't have it in her to try again. She re-tightened the scarf around her head, popped her third Rizact-5 of the evening, and closed her eyes. Sleep came late. Long after each of the thousand eruptions in her head had been capped one by one.

WED DECEMBER
17 **2014**

I

Leena remained unreachable. It wasn't new or unexpected, but Bindia worried a little more than usual.

Ashok wanted a tie for Sheena Chopra's party. There were a couple of things she could think of buying for the house and her body was begging for a massage. So Bindia went to The Palladium.

II

Tarun Dixit, Lucknow-based part-time insurance agent, called up younger brother Varun twice to remind him of the premium due on the Alto, found him unreachable.

THU 18 DECEMBER 2014

It was Sarlaji's birthday. She bathed early, applied an extra pinch of sindoor, slipped on the shiny green-and-red bangles picked especially for the occasion, and wore her husband's favorite green printed sari. Hariji made her morning tea, accompanied her to Sheetala Mata Mandir, slipped out briefly in the afternoon to get *atte ka laddoos* from Classic Sweets. She loved those, he knew.

In the evening, Tarun, Amita and the girls dropped by with cake and Coke. The girls surprised them with a longer, never-before-heard version of the 'Happy Birthday' song. Amita helped with the dinner and wrap-up.

The day went as it had in recent years. Except, Varun did not call.

Sarlaji kept the disappointment to herself. It was only after lights-out that she wondered aloud why the younger one hadn't called. Hariji informed her that Varun actually had. Early morning. She had been in the bath then. Varun had mentioned he would be in important meetings through the day, may not be able to speak to Ma later. The boy had been very, very apologetic, promised to call back as soon as work permitted.

Not entirely happy, Sarlaji nevertheless slept soundly that night. Her husband didn't. He had lied. Varun hadn't called. In fact, Varun's phone had been unreachable all day. Hariji had tried at least half a dozen secret reminder calls. Tarun when taken aside said Varun had been unreachable last evening too.

FRI DECEMBER
19 2014

I

Two early morning calls revealed Varun's phone as still unreachable. Retired Uttar Pradesh Police Sub Inspector Hari Dixit's third call was to a groggy Jalaj Saxena, the Gurgaon-based son of an old friend. Varun hadn't been taking calls recently. Aunty was worried. If it wasn't too inconvenient, could he have a look on the way to work? No, he was unlikely to be travelling. On rare occasions he did, Varun informed in advance, never switched off his phone, made it a point to call Aunty at least once a day from wherever he was.

Jalaj called back around 8.45 a.m. from somewhere in Pride Apartments. He had tried calling over the intercom from the security cabin at the gate, pressed the bell, hard-knocked, even shouted at the doors of A-403. There was no response.

Jalaj agreed to write down and follow-up on Hari Dixit's next questions, but it was clear from his tone that it was about all he would do.

Thirty minutes later, Hari Dixit learnt that:

- There were two newspapers outside Varun's door.
- The Alto was parked in the designated slot.
- Neither the security guards nor the neighbors had seen Varun recently.
- According to the security register, A-403 had had no visitors in the last few days.
- The guards wouldn't allow the flat to be entered without the owner or occupier's permission.
- Nobody available had the landlady's phone number. The office of the Pride Apartments Welfare Association (PAWA) would have to be approached for that.

Jalaj had been intelligent enough to collect the PAWA landline number. The PAWA Manager passed on the contact details of Mrs Sahni, Varun's landlady, after some persuasion.

Reached on the fourth attempt, around 11 a.m., Mrs Sahni turned out to be the helpful sort. She understood, she said, because she herself had a twenty-five-year-old living alone in another city. She did have a key but Mr. Dixit would appreciate she was in Delhi. It would take her some time to reach Gurgaon. Hari Dixit thanked her profusely, waited, hoped her husband or someone else did not dissuade her. He never came to know but her husband did – and was rebuffed.

II

For her maiden visit to a police station, Bindia avoided her preferred western wear, opted for minimal make-up and jewelry, remembered to carry the photograph and ID the helpful girl on 1091 had asked her to.

She went alone. Niti, her other good friend, had plenty on the plate already. Driver Pancham was not one to blabber, but with him, there remained the risk of Ashok finding out. It was best that her husband – travelling on work for the week, scheduled to return only for the weekend (his schedule after taking up the assignment in Mumbai about a year-and-a-half ago) – did not learn. Not at this point at least. He did not always understand reason. Rather her reasons.

Perhaps she would have waited some more had Ashok not been expected next morning. Perhaps she would have taken Pancham along had her destination not been sandwiched between a busy business hotel and a busier shopping complex.

She went with Pancham to the shopping complex, got him to park at the end farthest from the police station, cut through the complex on foot. At the station, the arrival of an unescorted, well-preserved lady created a mild flutter. Not long after, Bindia found herself before Station House Officer (SHO) Ajai Singh.

Though the potbellied, balding, mildly nasal Inspector – a mustached Satish Kaushik – remained polite through their conversation, his attitude irritated her. She was relieved when he finally passed her on to an underling 'to complete the formalities'. Had Bindia known better, she would have been grateful her complaint was admitted in the first place.

ॐ

With much to be done and precisely two semi-dependable men at his disposal, Ajai Singh liked to screen complaints thoroughly. In this case, a Daily Diary (DD) entry was unavoidable, given that it was a woman who was missing, but whether a full-fledged complaint was merited was another question. For several reasons.

First, the missing person was over eighteen.

Second, the informant admitted the missing person had dropped off the radar before.

Third, the informant was a friend, not a relative. As per the informant, the missing person had no family. Her parents were dead, there were no siblings and, if there had been a marriage, it appeared to have been childless and over. The women had re-established contact only recently, after a gap of more than twenty-five years. The missing person had moved to America when in school, returned a few months ago. Post-return, she had moved into the informant's spare apartment, generally been withdrawn and reluctant to discuss the intervening years.

The Inspector's final call was influenced not by the length of the missing person's absence or the informant's assurance that her friend was of sound mind, certainly not the sort to harm herself. The missing person's somewhat emotional state during her last meeting with the informant (a shopping expedition to Hauz Khas Village in Delhi) and the informant's mention of a puzzling late evening call received from the missing person, not long before her phone was switched off, couldn't be ignored though. The missing person had said something about going to settle an important matter once and for all. What the matter was, where she was going or who she was meeting had not been disclosed. Or asked.

In the main however, the Inspector's decision owed to the grave, determined manner of the woman who sat before him, the obvious fact that she was well heeled. A DD, Ajai Singh could see, wouldn't budge her.

౸

Fill in what you can here. The rest, Formality Desk said, he would.

MISSING PERSON FORM

<table>
<tr><td>Police Station: Vikrant Vihar</td><td>District: Gurgaon</td><td rowspan="3">(Paste missing person photograph here)</td></tr>
<tr><td>Missing Person Case No:</td><td>Dated:</td></tr>
<tr><td>DDR No.:</td><td>Date: Time:</td></tr>
</table>

1. INFORMANT

Name: Bindia Sehgal   **Parentage:** w/o Ashok Sehgal

Religion and Caste: Hindu, Khatri   **Address- House No.:** 204

Mohalla/ Colony: Elite Estates   **Village/ Town:** Gurgaon

P. S.: Vikrant Vihar   **District:** Gurgaon   **State:** Haryana

Age (years): 42   **Nationality:** Indian   **Phone No.:** XXXXXXXXXX

2. MISSING PERSON DETAILS

Missing from Place: Hauz Khas Village, Delhi (last seen)

Missing from Date: 16/12/2014   **Time:** 1.30 p.m. approx. (last seen); 8.15 p.m. approx. (last call)

Relationship with Informant: Friend, Tenant

Whether Mind Normal: Yes/ ~~No~~   **Whether Deaf:** ~~Yes~~/ No

Cloth Upper: Cream sweater*   **Cloth Lower:** Blue pants*

Foot Wearing/ Socks: Black shoes*   **Other Wearing:** Silver necklace, bracelet*

Last Seen Where, With Whom: Hauz Khas Village, Delhi; 1.30 p.m. approx.

*As last seen; also carrying Micromax phone (white cover) and black leather purse

P.T.O.

MISSING PERSON FORM   Page ii

---

3. MISSING PERSON PERSONAL DETAILS

Name: Leena Puri

Religion and Caste: Hindu, Khatri

Mohalla/ Colony: Platinum Heights

Passport No.:

Date of Passport Issue:

Parentage: d/o Late P. Puri

Address- House No.: C- 709

Village/ Town: Gurgaon

Place of Passport Issue:

Passport Valid Upto:

---

4. MISSING PERSON PHYSICAL DETAILS

Age (years): 42

Height (ft., in.): 5-2

Build: Normal/ ~~Fat/ Thin~~

Color of Eyes: Black

Face Type: Long/ Oval/ ~~Round/~~ ~~Sunken Cheek~~

Place of Burn Mark:

Place of Leucoderma Mark:

Peculiarities:

Sex: ~~Male~~/ Female/ ~~Transgender~~

Weight (kg.): 45-50

Complexion: Fair/ ~~Wheatish/ Dark~~

Color of Hair: Black (shoulder length)

Nose Type: Long/ ~~Bulbous/ Pointed/~~ ~~Snub (Pug)~~

Place of Mole/ Scar:

Place of Tattoo:

Any Other ID:

III

Mrs Sahni entered A-403 in the company of her driver, two security guards and the PAWA Manager. Her one p.m. shaky-voice call confirmed Varun was inside the apartment, dead.

I don't know how to say this, Mr Dixit. He is...he is...no more.

He is...you mean to say...?

I'm sorry, Mr Dixit.

No-no. How do you know? Who checked? You checked?

The guards are here. The PAWA Manager too. They went in with me.

They are sure? Sometimes people make mistakes about these things.

I...I don't know. I left them room as soon as I saw him on the sofa.

He could just be unconscious.

They seem sure about...things, Mr Dixit. The police have been informed.

How...I mean...how did he...? What happened?

They say he's been stabbed.

Murdered? They are saying he was murdered? They are saying he was murdered?

Yes.

The next question that came to his mind (Anything missing?) shamed him so much, he didn't ask it. Later, he would pin it on a one-time homicide investigator's reflex.

The rest of what Mrs Sahni said (*I'm sorry to be passing on such terrible news. I know it may not mean much at this point, but please do not hesitate to contact me if you need anything, anything at all.*) did not register.

Hariji slumped, closed his eyes in a brief prayer to Sai Ram.

How to tell Sarlaji? [Sarlaji, there is some bad news. About Varun.]

What, how much, to tell her? [He is gone/ is no more/ has left us forever. They are saying he was knifed.]

How would she take the news?

He heard the screams stuck in Sarlaji's chest. The first of those emanated at the sight of Tarun and Amita. The children, drawn early from school, cried because everyone around was crying. For what seemed a long while, each of them grieved independently, occasionally reaching out physically to comfort and be comforted.

Hariji was first to gather himself. There was a trip to plan.

Packing was quick, the earliest bus from Kaiserbagh taken. There was little point in the children travelling. Amita stayed back to be with them.

The journey was made in silence. Sarlaji and Tarun thought of Varun, how life would change after him. On Hari Dixit's mind was something else.

What had Varun done to invite murder? There had to be something.

Murder victims, unlike rape or theft victims, were never just victims, never completely innocent. Every single murder he had seen, even seemingly mindless ones, had revealed an ugly truth about the deceased – hurt, desperation and hopelessness in the killer.

So, what had Varun done to invite murder? There had to be something.

Truth be told, Varun had always had a malevolent streak. He had seen it in the humor-cloaked but unmistakably cruel mockery of the simple Tarun, the life-long manipulation of Sarlaji, the lustful glances cast at female cousins and neighborhood women, the cleverly disguised contempt for rules and his own straight ways.

And what had he done to stop, to change his son?

He wouldn't have lived to see this day if he had...done something.

He cried.

He cried some more.

SAT 20 **DECEMBER 2014**

Clarity came with dawn. To find his son's killer, he would have to be strong. Strong enough to confront his son's ugly side. Strong enough to not let guilt cloud his mind. There was no easier, nay other, way. Atonement could, would have to come later.

The rickety state transport bus rolled into Gurgaon. He disembarked at the foggy IFFCO Chowk ready to investigate his son's murder.

೮

Hari Dixit lingered over the mortuary register. The columns for name, date and time of death, details of near relatives informed, whether autopsy was carried out, date and time of autopsy, name of the autopsy surgeon and name of the person collecting the body were blank.

The sex (male), age (approximately 30), dimensions (72 inches in length, 44 inches across the shoulder), date and time when the body was placed in cold storage (19 December, 3 p.m.), identification marks (birthmark below right elbow) and list of valuables removed from the body (gold chain, stone-embedded gold ring, Fossil brand watch [blue dial, black leather strap], blue upper [full], grey vest, grey lower [full], brown underwear, white socks) were recorded in an untidy hand.

[Chain, ring, watch found on body. Approximate value: Rs 30,000 minimum. No robbery motive? Killer was known?]

Mahender, the person at the mortuary he had been asked to contact, unveiled the face slowly, then the rest of the body with complete lack of ceremony, and receded a few steps.

Hariji saw his dead son, the injuries that had claimed him, slowly ran his hand over the boy's forehead. It was the lone expression of affection he had known for his sons.

[Knifing. A gun would have been the practical choice for someone as strong as Varun. Killer not resourceful enough to arrange gun? Wound angles suggesting victim in inclined position. Killer strong enough to overpower then? Or cunning and close enough to sedate?]

There was an odd sense of relief. At least they had found a decent resting place, not left him in the open or stacked him inside the drawer with the mounting winter corpses. At least the putrefaction had been checked. There were three-day-old bodies he had seen in worse condition.

Ajai Singh saab has spoken to the doctor, he was informed without asking about something he knew already. *The post-mortem is due soon. The body can be taken late tonight, anytime tomorrow.*

Tomorrow, we will come tomorrow. Gurgaon is an unfamiliar city. A few people have to be informed. Arrangements have to be made. Where is the nearest crematorium?

Mahender retrieved two business cards from a wooden drawer, slid Varun back to his resting place, initially refused the small amount slipped into his hand.

Hariji returned to the cheap guesthouse where Sarlaji and Tarun waited, announced in the most matter of fact tone he could muster that the body would come tomorrow, passed on the crematorium numbers to Tarun, asked him to look for a slot around 11 a.m.

The first eye contact with Sarlaji since Mrs Sahni's call was to enquire if she was hungry. She wasn't. Neither was he. Food was arranged nevertheless.

SUN DECEMBER 21 2014

I

Varun Dixit was cremated around noon. Sarlaji, Tarun, Jalaj and a few of Tarun and Jalaj's friends attended. The ashes were collected in the evening. The family took the bus to Lucknow the same night. As before, Sarlaji and Tarun's thoughts turned to Varun. As before, Hari Dixit's mind was occupied with something different from his wife and son's.

The words of the post-mortem report burned in it.

II

The sub-contracted computer operator on the servant verification desk initiated the uploading of Leena Puri's details on the State Crime Record Bureau (SCRB) and the Zonal Integrated Police Network (ZIPNET) databases. With this, there was some action to show should the station at any point of time be accused of taking a missing woman's case lightly. The Sector 40 SHO had been suspended recently for not taking a kidnapping case seriously. With this, there would be breathing space to pursue other, more deserving matters. Like the four *charsis* who first tried to rob two rag pickers (boys aged eight and five), then raped and killed them out of disappointment.

Leena Puri, Ajai Singh would have maintained had he been asked, would return of her own accord soon. Modern, well-to-do women looked to disappear once in a while for some quality me-time. Many a Gurgaon policeman was familiar with such urges of *G4Glamor* readers.

MON DECEMBER
22 **2014**

I

Leena woke up in a dark room. 11:05 a.m., the clock said. From outside came the voice of a child thrilled at his mother's exasperated chase. It had to be a mother. An ayah would have used Hindi. Inside was the sadness-infused silence she had gotten used to.

Who would miss her, miss her enough to look for her, miss her enough to want her back? It was the question she had slept with. The answer remained unchanged: no one but Bindia. There never had been any family, not in a long time anyway. Friends and lovers she had always been unlucky with – though there were times she felt the problem may have been with her, not them.

She wasn't sure about Bindia either. For Bindia had other things in life to fall back on, occupy herself with. A family, a comfortable home, a wide friend circle. They counted. So what if the husband wasn't the most demonstrative, the son – a moody hosteller, the friends – shallow, gossipy, fair weather?

Come to think of it, it wasn't such a bad idea to leave Bindia. Withdrawing the emotional crutch would only do Bindia good. At least in the long run.

Everything hurt. Head, eyes, limbs. She felt hungry, very hungry. Would she ever see the world again, meet another person, make love, experience the thrill of a new dress or a nice meal? Who would miss her, miss her enough to look for her, miss her enough to want her back? Who?

It was time to do what she had attempted before. Disappear completely. Forever. Unlike before. The fan looked strong enough to hang from. If only she could get up. Till then, she would have to wither in this dark room. Or beg her captor for final release. Again.

II

Bindia woke up with a start. The question that she had slept with came to her. If she were to go missing like Leena, who would miss her, miss her enough to look for her, miss her enough to want her back?

Ashok, who made one ritual 8 p.m. call every weekday night on his way to the hotel gym? Jai, who hadn't spoken to her nicely in years? Her invalid father? Brother Param, who resented having to take care of Papa but wouldn't allow her near him either? The one true love that everyone except her seemed to have had? The bitches who called themselves her friends?

Friends she had always been unlucky with anyway. Except Leena. Why the hell did Leena have to go?

TUE 23 DECEMBER 2014

It wasn't the best time to leave. Sarlaji needed him, the stream of visitors hadn't died down completely, the *tehraveen* was coming up. Yet, Hari Dixit decided to make the trip to Gurgaon. Murder trails, experience told him, went cold quickly. Policemen, well-intentioned ones like Ajai Singh included, forgot quickly.

Once his mind was made up, Hariji convinced Sarlaji to stay with Tarun, asked Tarun and Amita to look after her while he was away. Never leave her alone for long. Before leaving, he withdrew Rs 30,000, his largest withdrawal ever. Half the amount was left with Tarun for the *tehraveen* arrangements, Rs 5,000 with Sarlaji who didn't quite understand what it was for.

Emergencies, he replied.

What emergencies?

Just keep it. Don't worry about anything. Call anytime you want to. Anyway, I will be back soon. Definitely a day or two before the *tehraveen*.

What about the tehraveen arrangements?

I am leaving money with Tarun. Ram Dutt Pandit is there to guide. There shouldn't be a problem. I will be available on the phone if they need me.

Sarlaji saw her husband off, dropped her head on Amita's shoulder once Tarun's scooter was no longer visible. Amita put an arm around her mother-in-law. The girls were with their friends in the park nearby. One of them sensed being observed, spotted her mother, directed the broadest smile at her as she came down the slide. Amita drew her mother-in-law close.

It's getting cold, Mummyji. Let's go inside. Should I make some tea?

WED DECEMBER 24 2014

I

[Scene: SHO's Office, Vikrant Vihar Police Station. The peeling pink walls have portraits of Gandhi (smiling) and Subhash Bose (stern, looking skyward), a crime-recording blackboard, a Haryana Government calendar, maps of Haryana State and Gurgaon district, pictures of wanted and missing persons. The blackboard and maps are fading; the pictures and calendar, frayed. The Inspector's desk is file-laden, as are the shelves lining the walls. All furniture – the Inspector's desk, his chair, the two chairs for visitors, the computer table, the chair for the computer operator and the shelves – is wooden, ancient. A rusty air cooler shuts off a sizeable part of the window behind the Inspector. The two tube-lights – switched on even though it's daytime – struggle to dispel the dark.]

[Ajai Singh is looking at a file. A constable dawdles in, stands behind a chair, says something inaudible. Ajai Singh looks up, returns to the file, signs and shuts it, hands it to the constable.]

Ajai Singh: Send him in. Remember to speak to Bipul Sharma at headquarters.

Constable: Sir.

[The constable leaves. Ajai Singh starts reading something on his phone.]

[Hari Dixit peeps through the curtain, waits for the Inspector to register his arrival, clears his throat as he steps in. Ajai Singh looks up, motions him to a chair, puts down the phone after a final glance. Through the conversation, Hari Dixit appears keen to find as much as possible and suggest lines of investigation without sounding imposing.]

Ajai Singh: You had to wait long.

Hari Dixit: No, not long. I understand you have much to attend to.

Ajai Singh: Things all right at home?

Hari Dixit: My elder son's there. There are relatives nearby. They will manage. I plan to return before the *tehraveen*.

Ajai Singh: When's that?

Hari Dixit: On 29th December.

Ajai Singh: It's in such times one realizes the value of family.

Hari Dixit: True, Inspector saab. I wouldn't have been here otherwise.

Ajai Singh: You are here to find if there's any progress? Some tea?

Hari Dixit: I had some just before coming.

Ajai Singh: Okay. First let us go over the things you may already know.

Hari Dixit: Ji.

[Ajai Singh fishes out a file from the pile on his desk, refers to it as he speaks.]

Ajai Singh: The post-mortem report you have seen. It puts the time of death between noon and 6 p.m. of 17th December, but both of us know it could be a few hours here and there. Some time elapsed before the body was found and the post-mortem could be conducted. What is clear though…

Hari Dixit: Inspector saab, I have information that could help narrow down time of death. I…I…can wait for you to complete or, if you want, share it now…whatever you think appropriate.

Ajai Singh: No-no. Go ahead. Say it now.

Hari Dixit: We spoke to him on the 17th around 2.30 p.m., 2.32 p.m. as per my phone call log. This was after hearing news of a bomb threat in Gurgaon on TV. We didn't speak long, just checked on his whereabouts and wellbeing.

Ajai Singh: I remember. HUDA City Center Metro Station. Turned out to be a hoax. What did he say?

Hari Dixit: That he was safe at home, not planning to go out. That's all.

Ajai Singh (glancing at the calendar): It was a…Wednesday – a work day. How come he wasn't in office?

Hari Dixit: Varun ran his own business, operated from home.

Ajai Singh: What business?

Hari Dixit: Event management.

Ajai Singh: Okay.

Hari Dixit (unfolding a piece of paper): Then Tarun, my older son, called him twice in the evening. At 7.07 p.m. and 7.46 p.m. Varun's phone was not reachable then.

Ajai Singh: That's as per the older one's call log?

Hari Dixit: Ji.

Ajai Singh: Time of death would be between 2.30 and 7 p.m. then.

Hari Dixit: Ji.

Ajai Singh: Anything else?

Hari Dixit: Nothing that comes to mind at the moment.

Ajai Singh: Coming back to the post-mortem report, death was caused by three stab wounds in the chest area. The wounds were caused by a single-edge knife. That kind of knife is commonly available. Nothing much to go ahead with there.

Hari Dixit nods.

Ajai Singh: There were no defensive wounds, no signs of forced entry. Which means the victim knew the killer. When you spoke to him, did he say he was expecting someone?

Hari Dixit: No. Only that he wasn't planning on going anywhere.

Ajai Singh: If I recall correctly, you made a family friend check with the security guards the day the body was found?

Hari Dixit: Jalaj, Jalaj Saxena. He's the son of a family friend. Lives in Gurgaon, works in a private company.

Ajai Singh: Our enquiries in that direction reveal nothing new either. As per the security register, the deceased had no visitors on or around the 17th. None of the neighbors saw anyone entering or leaving the flat either.

Hari Dixit: Ji.

Ajai Singh: We don't know how relevant it is going to be finally to the case, but we also found that the deceased didn't have visitors generally, leave alone any regular ones. The fourth floor neighbors remember running into him once in a while in the lift or the basement parking, but there appears to have been no contact between them beyond that. This limited interaction with neighbors may seem strange to people like you and me, but that's how it is in new Gurgaon.

Hari Dixit: The flat's been searched?

Ajai Singh: Yes. On Saturday.

Hari Dixit: I needed to collect his belongings.

Ajai Singh: No problem. We still have the keys. The owner family is out of station, supposed to return on the 29th. We can try calling them now itself.

Hari Dixit: Anything of note in the flat, Inspector saab?

Ajai Singh: A few things stood out. There was no sign of forced entry; the murder weapon wasn't around; the deceased's laptop and phone are missing; the only washed utensils in the kitchen were two tea mugs and other tea-making paraphernalia.

Hari Dixit: The tea mugs are…significant?

Ajai Singh: We think so. My guess is they had tea together. The killer cleaned the mugs later to remove fingerprints.

Hari Dixit: Ji.

Ajai Singh: I am also inclined to think that it was the killer who made the tea.

Hari Dixit: Why else would the tea-making paraphernalia be washed?

Ajai Singh: Correct. If the victim had made the tea, the killer would have cleaned only the cups.

Hari Dixit: Further confirms the killer was a known person.

Ajai Singh (a little dramatically): Also suggests the killer laced the tea with a sedative.

Hari Dixit: Oh.

Ajai Singh: The victim was strong, there were no defensive wounds and, above all, wound angles suggest he was slumped on the sofa at the time of knifing. Consider all this along with the fact that the killer made the tea and sedation becomes more than a possibility.

Hari Dixit (absently): Ji.

Ajai Singh: If I had to take out a strong person, I would use a sedative. Easy to get. Easy to administer. Mix in water if you wish. Victim can't make out anything. There's no smell, no taste, no color. Quick to take effect too. Fifteen minutes, maximum twenty. Do what you like after that.

[Awkward silence.]

Hari Dixit: Rapists use them a lot these days.

Ajai Singh: Oh, yes. Half – I'm not joking – half our rape cases are like that. Girl steps out with boy, has a soft drink, gets knocked out, wakes up raped by the boy and his friends, comes complaining.

Hari Dixit: Ji.

[Another awkward silence.]

Hari Dixit: Fingerprints were found?

Ajai Singh: You saw the article in today's paper?

Hari Dixit: No, sorry. What article?

Ajai Singh (with a hint of sarcasm): The Honorable Supreme Court is upset with Delhi Police for not handling fingerprints properly in crime scenes.

Hari Dixit (a tad defensively): I didn't know.

Ajai Singh: It was in today's *Rashtra Bandhu*. Anyway... there was a conscious attempt to clear fingerprints. Gloved hands have passed over surfaces. One more thing.

Hari Dixit: Ji.

Ajai Singh: Uh...I am sharing this with you only as an observation and...because I feel you should know.

Hari Dixit (puzzled): Ji?

Ajai Singh: The deceased had a rather – how do I put this? – extravagant lifestyle.

Hari Dixit: Extravagant?

Ajai Singh: Pride Apartments' residents are more than comfortable by any standards. Yet, we doubt if any of them could afford the kind of clothing, perfumes, etc., we saw in the flat.

Hari Dixit (after brief pause): Does it in any way link to the case?

Ajai Singh: Nothing to suggest that yet. It's only an observation, perhaps has no bearing on the case at all.

Hari Dixit: If there were no visitors, could it be a Pride Apartments resident?

Ajai Singh: Possible. Someone from Pride Apartments could indeed be responsible. Having said that, there's no evidence of the deceased's relations with any neighbor being so sour as to prompt an act like this. We asked around. All pointers are that there were no relations, good or bad, with any neighbor.

Hari Dixit: The murder weapon isn't in the Pride Apartments complex?

Ajai Singh: Not unless it was a resident who carried the weapon home. The common spaces were checked. We took the association's help. Nothing turned up.

Hari Dixit: Ji.

Ajai Singh: At the moment, we are inclined to think someone came from outside, went undetected. How, we don't know. This person, we can say with some surety, knew the deceased well.

Hari Dixit: They may have been in regular touch. The computer and phone wouldn't have been taken otherwise.

Ajai Singh: That occurred to us too. There was something in the laptop and phone that the killer either wanted for himself or did not want others to see.

Hari Dixit: We can find more about what was on the phone?

Ajai Singh: We will requisition call data records (CDRs) today-tomorrow. The cyber crime unit will look at it.

Hari Dixit: How long does it normally take them?

Ajai Singh: Can't say. They are a hopelessly overloaded lot. Getting the CDRs itself has become difficult after the Nitin Mahajan case. You know about it?

Hari Dixit: Ji, I've heard.

Ajai Singh: I don't know about your UP but the guidelines here in Haryana have been tightened a lot. Assistant Commissioner of Police (ACP) level approval doesn't work anymore. Higher-level approval has to be in writing. Statements of CDRs requested have to go to Chandigarh every month.

Hari Dixit: Oh.

Ajai Singh (sighing): In this country, rules, it would seem, are only for policemen.

Hari Dixit (maintains a diplomatic silence before changing tack): Anything unique about the glove prints?

Ajai Singh: No. Whatever experts say in meetings, trainings about glove prints, there never is much help there, is it? There's something else though that we plan to pursue in the coming days. We started talking on another point just when I was coming to it.

Hari Dixit: Ji?

Ajai Singh: While the flat itself was wiped clean, there was something in the car. The killer probably forgot, or didn't think it was important, to look there. Or did not want to risk venturing into the basement.

Hari Dixit: What?

Ajai Singh: A bill from an expensive Delhi nightclub called Spiff from the night before the incident, the night of 16th December. We plan to go there the day after.

Hari Dixit: Please don't take this otherwise but...but...is there a chance it could be done earlier?

Ajai Singh: Difficult. We are told they are busy with a promotional event for Aamir Khan's *PK* tonight and a Christmas party tomorrow. Christmas is Diwali Part II these days. The club owners are well connected. Best to tread carefully.

Hari Dixit: No, no, it's fine. Okay if I drop by on 26th evening then, after you have visited the club?

Ajai Singh: 27th morning would be better. The club opens only at night. We plan to go on 26th night. That way we can catch up with all the staff and, if needed, some of the regulars.

Hari Dixit (pausing between sentences): Okay. Inspector saab, thank you very much for all your effort. I...what to say... not everyone is so cooperative.

Ajai Singh: Dixitji, it's the least one can do for a fellow policeman. Make no mistake. We are going to nail the bastard who did it.

[Another awkward silence.]

Hari Dixit: If you can speak to the landlady...

Ajai Singh: Of course. How long do you think it's going to take in the flat?

Hari Dixit: If I get the key today, I can return it late tomorrow or first half day after. From what I know, it's not a large flat.

Ajai Singh (starts rifling through the desk): No, not large. You have the woman's mobile number somewhere?

Hari Dixit (locates the number on his phone): Ji. Here it is.

[Ajai Singh dials the number Hari Dixit reads out.]

II

Bindia Sehgal called, said her friend wasn't back yet, asked what the police was planning next.

Since there were no leads from SCRB and ZIPNET uploads, the next step would be a CDR requisition.

CDR?

Call data record, madam.

Oh, okay. When? It's been a week already.

We are planning to do it today-tomorrow.

When should I call again?

A week, ten days from now.

It will take that long?

Do understand, madam. We first have to get approval, then the phone company will send data, then we will look at it, then follow-up action will happen. All this takes time. What can we tell you before that?

Fine.

Do let us know if she returns in the meanwhile.

I will.

THU DECEMBER
25 2014

I

Hariji was scared to go inside A- 403. He felt a tightening in the stomach as he entered, sat on a chair to steady himself.
Old people die first, don't they, Papa?
Umm...yes.
That's why dada and dadi are dead, right?
Right.
Then, in our family, you will die first?
I guess so.
Then Ma, then Tarun bhaiyya. My turn will be last.
He held back the tears. Jalaj was at the door with cartons and help.

The Inspector was right. Varun hadn't had an ordinary life. Some of the stuff in the flat – the tall bar unit with bottles and glasses of all shapes and sizes, the coffee maker in the kitchen – was out of TV homes. Then there were the clothes, shoes, sandals, belts, watches, socks, underwear. Too, too many for a single person. The perfumes, lotions, shampoos, creams alone filled one large carton. He slipped the condom packets into that carton when no one was looking.

Wrap up took longer than anticipated. There was a brief break for lunch – tea, biscuits, samosas – Jalaj got from somewhere near. Through the day, Hari Dixit was reminded that his son's killer had roamed this very space. Here is where the tea was drunk. Here is where the mugs were washed. Here is where the computer was taken from. Here is where Varun fell. The killer would have skirted the body several times when cleaning up. Did the killer kick the body too?

What else had the killer removed besides the computer and phone? There was no way to find out.

Was there anything the police had missed, anything that could offer a clue to the killer's motivation or identity? There seemed to be none.

That was till he spied the only aged jar in the kitchen, opened it, found buried a small transparent plastic pouch between lumps of expired Horlicks.

Inside the pouch was the key to an Apex Bank locker.

Since it was hidden, it was likely to be hiding something.

Since it was hidden so carefully, it was likely to be hiding something important.

II

Bindia applied make-up while still in her bra, then slapped her thigh, pinched her sides, noted with satisfaction the less jiggle and less meat respectively, rolled sheer black stockings over her legs, donned the top and skirt.

The hair was being problematic again. She tried the bun, the pony and the loosening, leaned towards the bun, felt the need for a second opinion, missed Leena some more, decided to check with the lone soul available. Ashok was in town especially for

Sheena Chopra's party, and in a good mood too. Yes, it was that kind of event.

Ashok chose the bun. The thought of going another way just to spite him was dismissed as soon as it was admitted. The bun it was she carried that night.

The party was as happening as they had heard it would be. She spotted a supposedly gay TV news-show anchor acting contrary to reputation with a woman who seemed to be leaping out of her blouse, a sixty-something minor royal-cum-politician trying to score with a well-known forty-something fashion designer. The Santa for the evening, the ambassador of a vague East European country, got drunk, held aloft a twig he claimed was a mistletoe branch, insisted on kissing every female who passed by.

Sheena Chopra personally complimented her on her appearance, as did several others. The men couldn't stop staring at the leggy, under-clad Russian types (there could only be one reason they were there) and she concluded Ashok had been among them when he asked on the drive back home whether her panties were frilly.

Here then was a man who needed to know his wife of fifteen years better. She asked him to check for himself. Right now. The invitation took him by surprise, the finding more so. Going commando was meant to have been a private tribute to Leena, the one who had pointed her to pleasures unknown, unimagined, but what the hell?

FRI **DECEMBER**
26 **2014**

I

It took a while to find the branch where Varun had held his bank account. There Hari Dixit was told that the branch did not have locker facilities, the account holder had maintained a locker in another branch, revealing the location of the branch where the locker was held was not authorized. The branch manager would be the best person to talk to for further assistance. It was noon by the time the branch manager obliged.

Things didn't get better at the second branch.

Since the deceased depositor had not made any nomination and there was no will as the gentleman himself was mentioning, access to the locker could be granted only after a few formalities. A claim-cum-surety letter would have to be furnished in the specified format, along with a certified copy of the death certificate and a Succession Certificate/ Letter of Administration/ Probate of Will. A stamped receipt for the locker contents would be provided by way of closure.

Branch manager II repeated what client service executive II had said. *You have our deepest sympathies, but unfortunately, we will not be able to circumvent process. Please understand the position processing a request like this places us in.* Then added: *I can however ensure quick disposal of the matter when it comes to me.* Like he would have a choice after the paperwork!

The locker content then would have to wait till return from Lucknow. He was, he realized, acknowledging for the first time that there would be another trip to Gurgaon.

II

About five years ago, there was a suicide in a remote branch of our family. He returned home from college as usual, lunched, played carrom with his little sister and proceeded to jump off the neighboring railway bridge. They found his spectacles carefully folded and left behind at the point he jumped from. It was a strange thing to do, to think of preserving one's spectacles before squandering one's life.

The mother found the suicide note on his study table shortly after he left. That was when they started looking. By that time, he had done what he had to. Things might have turned out different had she found the note a few minutes earlier. Who knows?

The note was standard in most respects – contained an apology to the parents and the sister, a declaration that nobody but himself was to blame for the step – except one. It was typed. Meaning the decision wasn't sudden.

The captor was rambling again. She closed her eyes.

For the longest time, I blamed him for what happened. In my view, the act had been cowardly, selfish. Above all, avoidable. If only he had thought through his problems more carefully, spoken to someone in the family or, if circumstances demanded, approached the police or courts. All this was till my own troubles began, made me realize that circumstances sometimes leave no option but the most seemingly out-of-character, extreme one.

Now I understand why an outwardly happy young man from a caring, well-to-do family chose to commit suicide. You know what? There are at least five plausible scenarios I can imagine now which would have compelled him.

Stop it. Stop it.

The point I am trying to make, dear, is that circumstances sometimes prompt strange, desperate actions. The people who hear of those actions or bear the brunt of those actions never understand. No, that's not correct. They can understand if they put themselves in the other's shoes. You will too if you choose to stand where I am.

Silence followed.

She waited.

Silence still.

She opened her eyes slowly, looked around, saw no one.

She felt lighter.

Why?

The shackles were gone.

Only the heaviness of her own body, her own heart stopped her now. She picked herself with a small grunt, walked towards the window, drew the curtains, stared at the feeble afternoon sun, then drifted towards it.

Leena Puri left as secretly as she had arrived and lived. Exactly as she wanted. Exactly as her captor wished.

III

[Scene: Manager's cabin, Spiff. The wood-paneled cabin is neat but cramped, contains a small glass-top table, a swivel chair for the Manager, two leather chairs for guests. The walls are bare, but for a clock and an ash-streaked picture of a famous godman.]

[Someone escorts Ajai Singh in. The Manager rises to shake the guest's hands.]

Shubho Das: Hello, sir. Shubho Das. Manager here.

Ajai Singh: Inspector Ajai Singh. Gurgaon Police. SHO, Vikrant Vihar. We spoke earlier.

Shubho Das: I remember. Murder case.

Ajai Singh: Yes.

Shubho Das: Sorry, we couldn't accommodate earlier. The last few days have been very busy. I thought it best to meet here in my cabin. It's small but there will be no disturbance. Can I get you anything?

Ajai Singh: No, nothing.

Shubho Das: A drink maybe? I know you are on duty so won't press, but a mocktail maybe? Our mocktails are quite popular.

Ajai Singh: No, nothing. I'm fine. The man in this photograph was here on 16th December, found murdered the next day. We don't have much to go by except your bill here.

Shubho Das: Let me at the outset say that this establishment will cooperate with the police in every way possible.

Ajai Singh: Good to hear.

Shubho Das: Anything specific you wish to know?

Ajai Singh: This face is familiar to you?

Shubho Das: No, sir. This is a busy establishment. Moreover, in my position, I don't get to interact directly with guests.

Ajai Singh (reading from the bill): The bill mentions…Table 17…server S. Lal.

Shubho Das: That would be Sunder Lal. One of our waiting staff. Along with another waiter and myself, the oldest. Mind you, he's only twenty-five. In this line, no one sticks long.

Ajai Singh: Possible to speak to him?

Shubho Das: Of course. You may have to wait a bit though. He will be reporting a little late today. Someone unwell in the family. I'll ask for him to be sent over as soon as he comes.

[Shubho Das makes a call over the intercom.]

Shubho Das: Namita, send Sunder to my cabin as soon as he comes in. It's urgent. Okay?

[Shubho Das ends the call.]

Shubho Das: Done. They'll send him.

Ajai Singh (showing the bill to Das): This bill is for a single drink, was issued at 9.43 p.m.

Shubho Das (inspects the bill): Right.

Ajai Singh: Can we assume he was alone, left around 9.45-10 p.m.?

Shubho Das (handing the bill back to the Inspector): That would be the obvious conclusion but one can't be a hundred percent sure.

Ajai Singh: Why?

Shubho Das: So many reasons, Inspector saab. He could've been with a teetotaler or someone who was not in the mood for a drink. Or in company that decided to go dutch. Split, share the bill, I mean.

Ajai Singh: If they split the bill, there would be a bill for the same table at about the same time.

Shubho Das: Should be. That can be checked. Or he may have come alone, spotted an acquaintance, cleared the first bill, joined someone else on another table and that someone else may have handled the other bill. It happens. People come alone, run into someone they know, switch tables.

Ajai Singh: Means no certainty of 10 p.m. exit either?

Shubho Das: I'm afraid so.

[There's a knock at the door.]

Shubho Das: That would be Sunder. Should we call him in?

Ajai Singh nods.

Shubho Das (raised voice): Sunder? Come in.

[Sunder Lal enters, acknowledges the stranger in the room only after Das' introduction, stands throughout.]

Sunder Lal: Good evening, sir.

Shubho Das: Good evening, good evening. All well at home?

Sunder Lal: The doctor's asked for a few more tests.

Shubho Das: Oh. Get them done soon. Her problem's been going on for a while.

Sunder Lal: Sir.

Shubho Das: This is Inspector Singh from Gurgaon Police. He wants to ask a few questions. Cooperate with him, there's nothing to worry. No need to hide anything.

Sunder Lal: Sir.

Ajai Singh: Know this man in the picture?

Sunder Lal: Yes. He comes here frequently.

Ajai Singh: How frequently?

Sunder Lal: Once every ten-fifteen days.

Ajai Singh: Remember seeing him recently? On 16th December?

Sunder Lal: He was here some days ago. Whether it was the 16th I'm not sure. It was around that time.

Ajai Singh: He had a bill for the 16th. It mentions your name as the server.

Sunder Lal: Sir.

Ajai Singh: Basically, I'm talking of the night you saw him last.

Sunder Lal: Sir.

Ajai Singh: Was he alone that night?

Sunder Lal: There was a woman with him.

Ajai Singh: Who?

Sunder Lal: Don't know, sir. Not someone I remember seeing before.

Ajai Singh: How did she look?

Sunder Lal: I can't remember clearly, sir.

Ajai Singh: Can't remember *anything* about her?

Sunder Lal (after some thought): Fair, thin, short, I think. Short haired, maybe.

Ajai Singh: Anything unique you remember about her?

Sunder Lal (gives a blank look): —

Ajai Singh: Anything striking? Squint, bandaged hand, large bag, things like that.

Sunder Lal: No, sir. Sorry.

Ajai Singh: They came together? Left together?

Sunder Lal: I didn't see. I think she came after he did, left before him.

Ajai Singh: Why do you *think* that?

Sunder Lal: I remember him being alone when he placed the order. She wasn't around when he asked for the bill or when he paid for it.

Ajai Singh: Tell me something. You seem to remember this man rather well. How come? You must be serving many. I mean, there would be others who come once a fortnight or so?

Sunder Lal (casts a glance at Das, proceeds on Das' nod): He misplaced his phone here once, created a ruckus, accused one of the servers of stealing it, abused loudly. It was my first week on the job. I was shocked, expected people visiting a place like this to be more refined. After that incident, all waiters were wary of him. Most people from that time have left but Nandu will remember. His lady friend was upset too, nearly came to tears.

Ajai Singh (turning to Shubho Das): Nandu is the other senior waiter here?

Shubho Das: The one I told you about.

Ajai Singh (focus back on Sunder Lal): Something like that happened again?

Sunder Lal: No.

Ajai Singh: The phone was found?

Sunder Lal: Yes. Lodged between lounge cushions.

Ajai Singh: The woman he was with when the mobile got misplaced?

Sunder Lal: We didn't see her again.

Ajai Singh: Any particular person he talks to regularly?

Sunder Lal: No, sir. He stuck to the people he came with.

Ajai Singh: Who did he come with usually?

Sunder Lal (again awaits Das' nod before saying): There is a different woman almost every time.

Ajai Singh: Hmm, that'll be all. Let Manager saab know if you remember anything else about him or his companion that night. Or if she comes again.

Sunder Lal: Sir.

Shubho Das: Okay, Sunder, you can go. Remember what Inspector saab said. If you remember something else or see her again, tell me. Even if it does not seem important to us, it might be important for Inspector saab.

Sunder Lal nods.

Shubho Das: It's a murder case.

Sunder Lal (nods harder): Sir.

[Exit Sunder Lal. Ajai Singh and Shubho Das
watch him go, wait for the door to close.]

Ajai Singh: You have CCTV?

Shubho Das: Yes, we do and will be happy to provide the night's footage. I'm not sure how helpful it would be though.

Ajai Singh: Why?

Shubho Das: You see, Inspector saab, we, at Spiff, balance client privacy and safety concerns. Our cameras therefore cover only the entrance and toilet areas, not the core premises.

Ajai Singh: Core premises?

Shubho Das: Main club area.

Ajai Singh: Arrange the footage anyway. Maybe there'll be something there.

Shubho Das: No problem. We are talking about six-seven hours of footage from five cameras. Two at the entry. Three in the toilet area. More than thirty hours of viewing.

Ajai Singh: We are getting used to more these days.

Shubho Das: Arranging footage will take some time. It's good the requirement is not more than a month old. Else we would have overwritten the data.

Ajai Singh: How much time do you need?

Shubho Das: Today's Friday. By Sunday? We'll send it across. You need not go through the trouble of coming again.

Ajai Singh: Sunday is the 28th, right?

Shubho Das nods.

Ajai Singh: Fine. It has to be given to our station clerk Om Prakash. You can take down his number.

Shubho Das (picks a pen, opens a pad): Yes?

Ajai Singh: XXXXXXXXX. Got it? Make it early morning. The computer operator's with us only twice a week.

Shubho Das: There will be no delay on our part, Inspector saab. You need not worry.

[Brief pause.]

Ajai Singh: This thing about being with a different woman each time...

Shubho Das: Between you and me, Inspector saab, I wouldn't attach much importance to that.

Ajai Singh: Because?

Shubho Das: That happens often.

Ajai Singh: Here, you mean?

Shubho Das: Not only here, everywhere. Some men – why men, women too – don't have enough control.

Ajai Singh: You are saying he was...picking up women here?

Shubho Das: To be honest, I can't say no for sure. That's my personal view though. Off-the-record.

Ajai Singh: Off-the-record then, is it possible that the man was a male prostitute? I ask because his living standards were very hi-fi.

Shubho Das: What do I say, Inspector saab? There are many ways a man earns these days.

Ajai Singh (smiles): You are avoiding the question.

Shubho Das: He could've been one. Or he could've been someone's keep. One and the same thing. In many ways. Or he could have just been a man who enjoys the company of women.

Ajai Singh: One whose company women enjoyed too?

Shubho Das (smiles): People act of their own free will, Inspector saab. This establishment neither abets nor judges their actions. Please note that I am not saying he was into anything illegal.

Ajai Singh: What sort of women would they be?

Shubho Das: There are no identification marks, Inspector saab. Pardon me if it sounds tasteless but you'll see for yourself on the way out.

Ajai Singh: But one would have to be seriously loaded to think of entering this place.

Shubho Das: Oh, we are talking in that sense? Then I would add one would have to be clever too.

Ajai Singh: Clever?

Shubho Das: You cannot be discreet, successfully discreet that is, if you are not clever.

Ajai Singh (after a pause): He was the son a policeman.

Shubho Das: Oh. Rest assured, Inspector saab, this establishment will assist in every possible way. I have a small request though.

Ajai Singh: What?

Shubho Das: Do keep us informed of any developments likely to bear on this establishment's image. Our owner, Jatin Shah saab, is a public figure. Have you heard of him?

Ajai Singh: Who hasn't?

Shubho Das: Then you'll understand why he is mindful of reputational risk. This business is not even one-hundredth of the Shah Group, but you know how the media is these days. They wouldn't think twice before dragging a respectable man's name in the mud.

Ajai Singh: They'll relish it. I'll keep what you said in mind.

[Both rise, shake hands. Shubho Das holds the door as Ajai Singh exits.]

৪১

Spiff had warmed up by the time Ajai Singh left the Manager's cabin. He cast an eye on those present in the light of the last bit of conversation. The heavenly smelling middle-aged woman he had crossed could well be hunting for a lover for the night. The fresh-faced, well-built, well-groomed young man, at least ten years her junior, trying to catch her eye could well be the one she would choose. Or maybe not. There was no dearth of options here. For either of them. It didn't make Spiff a pick-up joint, but a joint where pick-ups happened it certainly was.

But why was he thinking on these lines? It had to be his own salacity, for the case wasn't pointing in that direction. In asking about men and women who hooked-up, what have you communicated about yourself to the Bangali Babu, you horny, low society bastard?

SAT DECEMBER 27 2014

[Scene: SHO's Office, Vikrant Vihar Police Station. The Inspector isn't at his desk.]

[Enter Hari Dixit, small travel bag slung over shoulder. He takes a seat, deposits the bag at the foot of the chair.]

[Enter Ajai Singh, wiping his hands into a handkerchief.]

Ajai Singh: Set to leave, Dixitji?
    Hari Dixit: From here itself. Here are the keys.

[Ajai Singh takes the keys, tosses them on the table, sits.]

Ajai Singh: We went to the club last night. One of the staff remembers seeing him on 16th night. He used to visit the place fairly regularly. Nobody remembers what time he came in or left that night, but there was a woman he was seen with.
    Hari Dixit: Has she been identified?
    Ajai Singh: Nobody remembers seeing her before. We are awaiting CCTV footage of the evening.
    Hari Dixit: When is it expected?
    Ajai Singh: They said tomorrow morning. I will ask the operator here to go through it first before sending to cyber crime. Otherwise there will be a long wait.

Hari Dixit: Hopefully there will be something useful there.

Ajai Singh: Let's hope. There's about thirty hours of footage and the operator's here only two days a week. Sundays and Tuesdays. If there's anything useful, it will not be before Tuesday-Wednesday that we will find it.

Hari Dixit: I'll be in touch.

Ajai Singh: I have saved your number, will call if anything comes up.

Hari Dixit: I'm thinking of coming back on Wednesday.

Ajai Singh: Dixitji, you really don't have to worry. We will take care of this. You are needed more at home.

Hari Dixit: My mind will be here even when I'm in Lucknow.

Ajai Singh: You know your situation better. What more can I say?

Hari Dixit: I'll take your leave for now, Inspector saab.

[Hari Dixit picks the travel bag, exits. Ajai Singh watches him leave.]

SUN DECEMBER
28 2014

I

The station clerk handed Varun Dixit's photograph and the CCTV footage to the computer operator, repeated the Inspector's instructions.

- Look through the footage, find what time the man in the photograph entered the club, what time he left, what time he re-entered and re-left. Print the picture of every person he was seen approaching/ approached by/ together with/ talking to, including club staff.
- The priority is pre-10.30 p.m. footage from the entrance camera. Post-10.30 p.m. footage and footage from other cameras is to be examined later, obviously only for time slots when the man was inside the club. The idea is to get something to chew on before Wednesday morning.
- Call Inspector saab on his mobile if there's any confusion.

Before leaving for the day, the operator informed the station clerk over the phone that he had been able to go through about half the footage, established the man's time of entry and exit, found no individual in his company, left four time-stamped photos on the Inspector's desk.

What the operator left unsaid, partly because the station clerk did not ask, partly because it was late, was that Varun Dixit appeared in only two of the four. The other shots were of the woman whose details he had uploaded the previous Sunday. Leena Puri.

II

Ashok slept off in the middle of *Comedy Nights with Kapil*. Bipasha Basu and Karan Singh Grover were screwing the only half-decent show on desi TV. She, though not sleepy herself, shut off the lights and TV, watched him in the light straining from the curtain cracks. Grey on temples, moustache and chest, mouth slightly open, distended stomach going up and down, toes peeping from below the blanket.

Bindia felt a surge of affection, cuddled up from behind. He turned, pulled her close, breathed into her face. In another time, she would have lifted her top, pressed her breasts against his chest, been tickled by the tumescence on her thigh. Tonight, she was content with just the proximity, wanted it to remain asexual.

It had been a long day. Spent shopping, lunching with old friends Pratima and Chetan, preparing dinner together, dusting out the Scrabble board. All his ideas. She wasn't going to fault him for trying. Not since the Christmas party. How remedying sex could be!

Leena wafted in at some point of time, was shooed away.

Not tonight, please. I'm surprised, ashamed at how well I am coping without you. Guess it's got to do with the fact that you were – our relationship was – a secret. It's the good thing about keeping something hidden from the world. When it's lost, nobody else misses it. Because, for the world, it never existed. Which means the secret-keeper is forced to act, learn to live as if it never existed. That is why I act, am learning to live as if you never existed. Doesn't mean I don't miss you. You should know I do. A lot. But not tonight, please.

Please.

Leena didn't relent.

Tomorrow then? Once Ashok's gone?

Leena obliged.

Tomorrow was going to be trying in so many ways.

MON **DECEMBER**
29 **2014**

The *tehraveen* guests came from Allahabad, Barabanki, Hardoi, Kanpur and, of course, Lucknow. Stationed at the entrance, Hariji avoided their pity-loaded eyes, accepted their mumbled same-sounding condolences, ushered them into the house, checked the *halwai*'s progress from time to time, ticked off the accumulating beggars for being impatient and not allowing the guests to pass through. The ladies occupied a separate section behind Sarlaji, who kept her head bent throughout.

Tarun and Amita sat for the *pooja*. Ram Dutt Pandit presided. All present tried to maintain an occasion-befitting expression, failed, ended up betraying signs of boredom. Some stifled yawns, others checked phones, yet others absorbed themselves with durrie lint. The relatives registered presences and absences, arrivals and departures.

Big relief: If there was speculation, it certainly wasn't verbalized aloud. One or two of Hariji's ex-colleagues who broached the matter restricted themselves to asking about the Gurgaon police's progress with the case.

Bigger relief: Sarlaji held up.

People ate well, left in trickles. After the last guest left, the bereaved couple sat next to each other, stared into the distance and sipped tea in silence.

Hariji wondered if it was the right time to bring up his Gurgaon plans. Sarlaji wondered how long it would be before her husband brought up his Gurgaon plans. Closing the case wouldn't bring her son back, but it would her husband. Maybe.

TUE 30 DECEMBER 2014

Shubho Das: Hello. Inspector Ajai Singh?

Ajai Singh: Speaking. Who is that?

Shubho Das: Shubho Das this side, Sir. From Spiff. You got the CCTV footage?

Ajai Singh: On Sunday itself. The operator looked through half of it on Sunday, should complete the rest today.

Shubho Das: Anything useful?

Ajai Singh: Don't know. I haven't had the time to check. VIP duty, court appearances. How come you called?

Shubho Das: There's something we came across last night. I thought it might help.

Ajai Singh: What is it?

Shubho Das: One of our guests, a male, was observed filming a lady guest on his mobile phone last night. We don't tolerate such things and the concerned person was asked to leave the premises. The phone was returned to him after deleting the offending video. We offered to call the police, but the lady in question didn't want to escalate the matter.

Ajai Singh: Okay?

Shubho Das: When checking the phone, we found a few other clips shot on our premises. One of them was from 16th December.

It shows the man you were asking about and the woman he was with. We have saved the clip. You have WhatsApp? I can send it right now.

Ajai Singh: Yes, do that. It's good you called.

Shubho Das: Our civic duty, Inspector saab.

WED DECEMBER
31 **2014**

Photographs, CCTV footage and WhatsApp video seen, Ajai Singh pieced all he knew so far about the evening of 16th December in his head.

෪

8.13 p.m. [Call received by Bindia Sehgal from Leena Puri]

Leena Puri says she is going to settle an important matter.

8.53 p.m. [CCTV footage, Entrance camera]

Varun Dixit enters Spiff alone. He is in a dark blue shirt of slightly shiny material, black pants.

8.59 p.m. [Order data from Spiff]

Varun Dixit occupies Table 17, places an order with Sunder Lal. Sunder Lal remembers Varun Dixit being alone on the table at this point.

9. 24 p.m. [CCTV footage, Entrance camera]

Leena Puri enters Spiff alone. She is in a chocolate-colored knee-length full-sleeved dress, carries a dark brown purse.

9.28 p.m. [WhatsApp video]

Leena Puri and Varun Dixit are sharing Table 17. Sunder Lal has delivered the order. (A near full drink rests before Varun Dixit.) The video zooms onto Leena Puri's calves, shifts instantly onto her thighs as if the zoom onto the calves was a mistake, lingers there, goes on to soak in her tummy and breasts, concludes.

9.32 p.m. [CCTV footage, Bathroom camera]

A woman appears briefly in the corridor leading up to the ladies' bathroom, does not enter it, instead turns around and disappears back into the club. Only her back can be seen but its clear from the clothes and purse that it's Leena Puri.

9.35 p.m. [CCTV footage, Entrance camera]

Leena Puri exits Spiff, looks back at someone or something before dissolving into the night. She doesn't approach a valet or ask for a taxi callout.

9.43 p.m. [Bill for Table 17]

Varun Dixit gets his bill. Sunder Lal remembers him being alone on the table.

9.57 p.m. [CCTV footage, Entrance camera]

Varun Dixit exits Spiff. The valet is not approached, nor a taxi called. He drove himself. How else would the bill end up in his car?

ॐ

- Varun Dixit and Leena Puri knew each other (?).
- Differences emerged between them over time (?). Leena Puri, going by her call to Bindia Sehgal, was hoping to do something (decisive?) about those on the night of 16th December (?).
- They met briefly that night. Leena Puri was at Spiff for all of eleven minutes, spent not more than five with Varun Dixit. It looked as if she made an excuse about going to the bathroom (therefore walked in the general direction of the bathroom but did not use it), left secretly without returning to the table (her exit from the club was within three minutes of being captured on the bathroom camera). When she looked over her shoulder before leaving, it was perhaps to ensure that he wasn't following (?). It was, currently, the last known sighting of her.
- After a wait of about ten minutes, Varun Dixit realized she wasn't coming back, asked for the bill. He drove away himself, was found murdered the next day.
- Someone must have definitely seen Leena Puri after her exit from Spiff. Either a parking attendant or a taxi driver or an acquaintance.

If it was a parking attendant, he may remember. Not too many women came alone to a place like Spiff and self-parked at that distance.

If it were a taxi driver, he would've been in wait at a specified spot, someone known, trusted. The search for such a driver was best started at a taxi stand near her home.

If it was an acquaintance, who was it? And could it have been the acquaintance waiting in the car – not Varun Dixit – that

Leena Puri had set out to settle matters with? Had her encounter with Varun Dixit then been a chance one?

Of course, Leena Puri's call to Bindia Sehgal, short visit to – and sudden flight from – Spiff could have been about something else altogether, something completely unrelated to Varun Dixit or his murder but this, for the moment, was the most credible plotline that Ajai Singh could think of. And, as all policemen knew, behind every crime was a plot, behind every successful crime investigation, its unraveling.

Old Man Dixit would be coming today-tomorrow. Ajai Singh was glad he had something for him, made a mental note of things to be done next:

- Ask for CDR analysis to focus on calls between Varun Dixit and Leena Puri.
- Ask operator to finish viewing remaining CCTV footage.
- Speak to Spiff parking attendant.
- Speak to Bindia Sehgal.
- Search Leena Puri's residence, car.
- Speak to taxi stands near Leena Puri's residence.

It would all have to wait though. For tonight was high alert. To ensure that merrymakers did not get too drunk, too frisky. Essentially, too merry.

THU JANUARY
01 2015

I

Breakfast-in-bed was a romantically unimaginative gesture exalted by romantically unimaginative admen. Messy too. She hated it. Still Bindia had to appreciate what Ashok placed before her. Everything was the way she liked. Eggs: Scrambled. Toast: Crisp, smeared with both butter and orange marmalade. Coffee (being the first of the day): Strong, milky, sugary. Though bloated from the excesses of the hotel party, they were hungry.

Ashok removed the tray once she was done, returned to kiss her. A certain dryness, the smell of alcohol lingered in their mouths. No matter.

Ashok Sehgal: Want to wish us?
Bindia Sehgal: I thought I already did.
Ashok Sehgal: He doesn't remember.
Bindia Sehgal: Too bad.
Ashok Sehgal: He'll be sad.
Bindia Sehgal: And you?
Ashok Sehgal: I'll manage. But you got to feel for him.
Bindia Sehgal: You mean feel him?
Ashok Sehgal: Whatever. Just be nice to him.

Bindia Sehgal: Okay then. Come here, my Ashik. Don't you feel bad. Come. Let me kiss you. Here. Fine? Happy?

Ashok Sehgal: Hmm.

Bindia Sehgal: I see he's feeling better already.

Ashok Sehgal: Yes.

Bindia Sehgal: Why you crying, my Ashik?

Ashok Sehgal: Tears of joy.

Bindia Sehgal: Happy New Year, Ashik. And Happy New Year to you too, Ashok.

Ashok Sehgal: Umm.

II

FORM OF INVENTORY OF ARTICLES
LEFT IN THE LOCKERS

The following inventory of articles left in lockers with <u>Vikrant Vihar- Phase II</u> branch of Apex Bank by Shri/ ~~Smt.~~ <u>Varun Dixit</u> (deceased) under an agreement/ receipt dated <u>12/9/12</u> was taken on this <u>1</u>st day of <u>January 2015</u>.

S. No.	Description of Articles	Other Identifying Particulars, if Any
1.	Case containing two CDs	Transparent, unmarked CD case with two CDs; both CDs carrying the number- XXXXXXXXXX

The above inventory was taken in the presence of Shri/ ~~Smt.~~ <u>Hari Dixit</u> (Nominee/ Legal Heir) or Shri/ Smt. <u>Not Applicable</u> (Guardian appointed on behalf of Minor Nominee/ Legal Heir) and Shri/ Smt. <u>Not Applicable.</u>

Address: <u>C- 154, Krishna Colony, Aliganj, Lucknow 226024</u>

Signature: _____

I, Shri/ ~~Smt.~~ <u>Hari Dixit</u> (~~Nominee/~~ Legal Heir/ ~~Guardian appointed on behalf of Minor Nominee/ Legal Heir~~) and Shri/ Smt. <u>Not Applicable</u> (Survivor only in case of joint holding) hereby acknowledge receipt of the articles comprised and set out in the above Inventory together with a copy of the said Inventory.

Date and Place: <u>1/ 1/ 2015, Gurgaon</u>

Signature: _____

Signed and sealed in the presence of:

Name and signature of Branch Official 1: _____

Name and signature of Branch Official 2: _____

Jalaj loaded the CD, showed Hari Dixit the play button, waited outside as instructed, came in to load the second CD, waited outside again.

The CDs had the same content: a fully naked woman, asleep, every inch of her captured slowly with focus on identity marks. Hariji couldn't bring himself to watch it closely, didn't know what to make of it.

Had Varun filmed it secretly? For what? Kicks? Blackmail? If it was a secret filming, the woman had motive for murder. If it was a secret filming, the Inspector must know.

But what if it was a consensual filming? There would then, in the end, only be disgrace for his late son and the woman concerned, embarrassment for the Dixit family, time wasted barking up a wrong tree.

The woman was either a victim or a murderess. As a victim, his son's victim, she needed balm, closure. As a murderess, his son's murderess, she needed to be probed. Neither could happen till she was contacted. Thankfully, there was a phone number- and a hook. Victim or murderess, there would be interest in the CD.

The initial contact would be made in personal capacity. Nothing illegal in a father wrapping up his deceased son's affairs.

Jalaj was playing some game on his mobile when he stepped out.

Anything else, uncle?

You've done enough already, beta. Go now. Get on with your day.

Hari Dixit decided to get the boy a nice watch once it was all over.

FRI 2 JANUARY 2015

Hari Dixit: Hello.

Female voice: Yes?

Hari Dixit: XXXXXXXXX?

Female voice: Yes. Who's this?

Hari Dixit: Madam, my name is Hari Dixit. You may know my son Varun, Varun Dixit.

Female voice: No, I don't.

Hari Dixit: Varun Dixit. Late Varun Dixit.

Female voice: Sorry, I don't know anyone with that name.

Hari Dixit: Madam, my son passed away recently. While packing his belongings, I came across something that belonged to you, and wanted to return it.

Female voice: The name doesn't ring a bell.

Hari Dixit: Your number was mentioned on the package.

Female voice: Some confusion.

Hari Dixit: Hello. Hello?

[Hari Dixit dials again.]

Hari Dixit: Sorry madam. We got disconnected.

Female voice: I had disconn…Sir, I'm busy. I told you I don't know anybody of the name you mention. No question of him having something that belonged to me.

78

Hari Dixit: Try to remember, madam. Please. You may have known him around 2012.

Female voice: 2012 you said?

Hari Dixit: Ji.

Female voice: My predecessor here at NimbleSoft had this number in 2012.

Hari Dixit: Can I speak to your predecessor then? What my son left may be valuable to the person.

Female voice: She's no longer in the country. Moved to Australia after leaving the company. We haven't been in touch. She might be somewhere else now for all I know.

Hari Dixit: Oh. Is there any way I can reach her?

Female voice: I may have her personal e-mail id somewhere. Not sure if she still uses it though.

Hari Dixit: Anything you can provide will be helpful.

Female voice: Hold on a sec. You sure there's no hanky-panky here Mr errr?

Hari Dixit: Dixit. Hari Dixit. I am a retired...government servant, madam. Trying to close my late son's affairs. There is nothing mala fide, believe me.

Female voice: Okay. Found it. Take it down.

Hari Dixit: One minute. Yes?

Female voice: It's minnakumar_33@xxxxx.com. That's m for monkey, i for India, double n, n for nose, kumar, underscore, the number 33 at xxxxx dot com. Got it?

Hari Dixit: Yes. Thank you, madam. This is a great help.

Female voice: Hope there isn't going to be any trouble.

Hari Dixit: Be assured, madam. I am only trying to return something that belonged to Minnaji.

Female voice: What did you say your son's name was?

Hari Dixit: Varun Dixit.

Female voice: And you are?
Hari Dixit: Hari Dixit.
Female voice: Okay.

※

From: Sampada Seth
Date: Fri, 2 Jan 2015 10:33:11 +0530
To: Minna Kumar
Subject: Someone called Hari Dixit called

Hey M.

Long time. How are you guys doing? In Oz still?

Just wanted to let you know that one Hari Dixit called for you earlier today. Said his son Varun passed away recently, left behind something important for you. Sorry, I didn't ask what it was. You know how the day is here! Zook's still alive ;-).

The guy wants to get it across to you, wanted your contacts. It sounded urgent so I passed on your xxxxx id. Hope that's fine.

Best,
Sampada

※

From: Minna Kumar
Date: Fri, 2 Jan 2015 17:17:35 +1100
To: Sampada Seth
Subject: Re: Someone called Hari Dixit called

That's cool, Sam. Wonder who this is though??

Yup, still in Oz. Chilling after all those years. Hubz doing the grunt work. For a change ;-).

Hear you are going places at NS, Zook notwithstanding. Touchwood!

Keep in touch.

Best,
Minna

❦

The mail took Hari Dixit a while to draft. The final version deliberately:

- Omitted any reference to his police past. It would only have scared the woman.
- Did not mention Varun's murder. If she knew about it sitting in Australia or wherever, there would be good reason to suspect her involvement.
- Did not mention what important thing he was holding. It was worth seeing if she knew about the CD.
- Included a phone number. A person in her situation may not want to reply in writing.

৪০

From: retdpsi_haridixit@xxxxxx.com
Date: Fri, 2 Jan 2015 23:41:20 +0530
To: minnakumar_33@xxxxx.com

Subject: Return of your property held by late Varun Dixit

Dear Madam,

I, Hari Dixit, am the father of Varun Dixit. Varun expired recently. While gathering his belongings, I came across something of yours he had held. How do I return the same to you? I think it may be important to you. Please let me know at the earliest. My mobile number is XXXXXXXXXX.

Yours sincerely,
Hari Dixit

SAT 3 JANUARY 2015

[Scene: SHO Ajai Singh's Office, Vikrant Vihar Police Station.]

[Hari Dixit stands at the door, knocks. Ajai Singh is referring to numbers from loose papers, punching them into a calculator, taking down the results on a separate sheet.]

Hari Dixit: Come in, Inspector saab?
    Ajai Singh: Come, come. Everything went okay?

           [Hari Dixit enters, takes a seat.
    Ajai Singh continues with the number crunching.]

Hari Dixit: Yes. All went well.
    Ajai Singh: Good-good. One minute.
    Hari Dixit nods.

           [Ajai Singh stops after a few seconds.]

Ajai Singh: When did you return?
    Hari Dixit: Thursday itself. Got busy closing my son's bank account after that.
    Ajai Singh: We found a few things in the meanwhile from CCTV footage and talking to a few people.

Hari Dixit: Ji.

Ajai Singh: It's confirmed Varun Dixit was at Spiff between 9 and 10 p.m. on 16th December. He was joined by a woman for about five minutes, around 9.30 p.m. Neither returned to the club later. She herself has been missing from that night onwards.

Hari Dixit: Oh.

Ajai Singh: The last call she made to the informant in her case was around 8.15 p.m. the same day. Said she was going to settle something important once and for all.

Hari Dixit: Anything else she mentioned?

Ajai Singh: No, nothing. The informant didn't press either. Was busy trying to get through to her son at boarding school. That was the day of the Peshawar school attack.

Hari Dixit: Right, right.

Ajai Singh: However, given that she met Varun Dixit that night, left within minutes of meeting him and completely disappeared after that, there's a chance the two cases are linked.

Hari Dixit: She's not been seen since at all?

Ajai Singh: She didn't use a valet, call for a taxi or drive herself. The parking attendant doesn't remember someone of her description. When the informant called her around 10.30 p.m., her phone was switched off.

Hari Dixit: Bodies matching description?

Ajai Singh: Nothing so far. We put up the notice long ago.

Hari Dixit: Someone was in wait for her outside the club then?

Ajai Singh: I am thinking a taxi or an acquaintance. The club's in Delhi, her residence in Gurgaon. If it were a taxi, it may have been taken from a stand near her home. Things would be more complicated if it was an acquaintance. All sorts of questions come into play then.

Hari Dixit nods, but checks himself from saying something.

Ajai Singh (sensing the unsaid request): We plan to visit the missing woman's residence on Monday, will show her picture in the nearby taxi stands then.

Hari Dixit: Ji.

Ajai Singh: Today's not possible. Everyone's tied up. We are yet to talk about the keys with the landlady. The landlady, by the way, also happens to be the informant. Apparently, the missing woman had no family. You want to join us on Monday?

Hari Dixit: Ji, Inspector saab. You will not be inconvenienced.

Ajai Singh: Fine. We will leave around 10.30 a.m.

[The phone rings. Ajai Singh takes the call, waves in acknowledgment of Hari Dixit's parting gesture.]

SUN 4 JANUARY 2015

*T*hey first met at Ale+. Minna spotted him across the floor, liked what she saw, made her move straightway. There wasn't much time. Plus, guys like him – tall, athletic, well groomed – weren't short of takers. Not on singles' nights at Ale+. It wasn't too difficult to make out who was hunting and who wasn't, but she used the established opening line for confirmation nevertheless.

What's your size and girth? Enough, he replied. To someone who blinked at the question, which meant someone who wasn't in the game so to speak, the repeat would have been 'what's your sign of birth'. They waited till he finished his drink, moved to the hotel room upstairs.

Minna normally did not book rooms herself, but it was a particularly hungry night. Of course, she had remembered to wear something not too flashy (the switch to the slutty, Ale+ appropriate look had been in the room), use a taxi, pack a small suitcase, enter a false name (the first name of one colleague, the surname of another), address (of a cousin who had moved cities) and phone number (an old number of Vaibhav's with the last three digits jumbled), pay cash advance. The sweetly delivered lie about having forgotten the ID worked.

86

After sex, they exchanged numbers and she set the future meeting rules.

- *He was never to call, text or ask personal questions.*
- *Suggestions on sexual acts were welcome, but the final decision would be hers and hers alone.*
- *All future meetings would be held on dates, in time slots she would indicate.*
- *From her side, she would try to ensure reasonable advance notice, connect with him to confirm final arrangements.*
- *His job was to make all bookings and payments for which he would be reimbursed in cash.*

The sex itself hadn't been the best she had had, but not the worst either. He had made a big ceremony of the undressing, lingered a little too long over the earlobes and generally been less rough than she liked, but there was potential.

The feedback, which she was always open about with all her lovers because coyness would never get the bang for the bucks she was shelling, was well received. It was the reason she was readying herself for their fourth encounter. A record of sorts because most people never listened, because she was clear about not acting as a finishing school for mediocre lovers.

At the hotel on MG Road, she marched straight to the guest lifts. No hotel staffer asked anything. It was one of the advantages of being – and looking like – a well-to-do woman.

He was waiting. Pajamas only. The initial rituals were established. First came the joke. (Ready to earn your hardship allowance? See for yourself. Hmm.) Next, the beer, which they sipped sitting opposite each other. The rest was a blur.

She would discover what happened that afternoon a few days later. Via a video where she saw herself naked, a cleverly shot video that left no doubt it was her. Her face, her body. The bastard had filmed the moles on the inner thigh and right boob.

She saw the video only once, paid for it a long time, prayed everyday for his end.

Now, this mail. Nearly three years later, nearly three years after she was forced to leave the country, nearly three years of keeping it in her pants.

All sorts of questions swirled in her head. Was this Hari Dixit really Varun's father? Was Varun really dead? Was the CD the important thing he claimed to have? Could it be something else she hadn't known of so far? What could *that* be? Did this person actually intend to return the CD or whatever else it was that he was holding? Was this bait for another round of blackmail, by another person? What if it was Varun who was claiming to be Hari Dixit? The lowlife was capable of that.

Once Shivam and Vaibhav went golfing, she dug into the cupboard, recovered the cigarettes she hadn't touched since July, lit one. This was an emergency situation if ever there was one. The conversation with herself ended with the stubbing of the second Longbeach.

ॐ

Relax, Minna. Think through this. A mind clouded with questions isn't going to yield answers.

Yup. Yup, I get that.

What's your chief worry?

Being blackmailed again. Being exposed if I refuse to play ball.

What will make your worry go away?

Getting hold of the CD, whatever else there is. Destroying it with my own hands.

How do you get hold of what he has?

First, confirm what he has, then ask for it. Is there any other way?

You plan to get in touch with him then?

Yes. Not on e-mail. Over public phone. Why does that surprise you?

Because you can ignore the mail. This person's probably in India, you are far away, he probably doesn't know where. If he is Varun's father, he will be old, will tire after a point.

If he is Varun's father. That's a big if, isn't it? What if it's Varun? What if it's someone else, not Varun's father? Varun is more than capable of releasing the video. If it's someone else, they could too. They've got nothing to lose.

What if it *really is* Varun's father?

Varun's father, I am not sure of either. Varun could well have inherited the evil gene from him.

You are saying the risk in going quiet is very high, there's no option but to talk.

Yup.

You think he's going to give you whatever he has simply on asking?

No. I don't know. Maybe. But I need to find what he wants in return. Whoever he is. Varun, his father, someone else.

What if it turns out to be Varun or another blackmailer? That's no solution to your worries either.

Right. My comfort currently comes from the physical distance, the fact that he has only discovered an e-mail id.

What are you going to tell him?

I am hoping to keep it simple. Ask what he has, what he wants in return. But before that satisfy myself about Varun's death, him being Varun's father.

That may mean more than one conversation.

Then there will be more than one public phone.

MON JANUARY
5 2015

Minna sat before the computer, began her sleuth work with two names (Hari and Varun Dixit), the mobile number mentioned in the e-mail and a piece of information received once in passing (that Varun's father was a retired cop living in Lucknow).

A plain Google search on Varun Dixit revealed nothing notable beyond what she had seen in her last quarterly search for that name. If Varun Dixit was dead, Google didn't know it. No Lucknowite of probable age was thrown up with Hari Dixit. Truecaller did not have a record of the mobile number. All that could be gleaned was that it belonged to a subscriber from Western UP.

Not productive so far.

The name search option on the website of the UP Chief Electoral Officer showed two Hari Dixits in their sixties in Lucknow district. She took down their details – name of father, name of Assembly Constituency, part number of Assembly Constituency, Electronic Photo Identity Card (EPIC) number.

A deeper dig on the same site with those details and she knew that only one of the two Hari Dixits had a son named Varun. She also found the correct Hari Dixit's date of birth, postal address, spouse name and names of his two immediate neighbors. That one of neighbors was a middle-aged widow (Kamla Prasad, w/o of Late Birender Prasad) living with a twenty-three-year-old son (Nitin Prasad, s/o of Late Birender Prasad) gave her an idea.

The pensioners' list on the UP Police website provided Hari Dixit's date of retirement. Feeding Hari Dixit's name and date of birth on the e-filing portal of income tax provided his Permanent Account Number (PAN). BSNL's online directory provided the landline numbers of the Dixit residence and the widow.

She left home around 2 p.m. Australian Eastern Daylight Time. Two calls were made from two different public phones. The second was to Hari Dixit.

She made it in time to Shivam's school bus stop.

৪৩

Kamla Prasad rushed to the phone, worried the ring would wake up Nitin. The woman calling was a relative of the Dixits from Kanpur. The Dixits hadn't been picking the house phone the last few days, she somehow had this number, was calling to find if everything was fine with them. Kamla informed the caller that the Dixits had been in and out since the younger one passed away, advised her to try Hariji's mobile number. The woman sounded shocked at the news, confirmed if it was Varun Kamla was talking of and took down the mobile number. The call got disconnected thereafter. Kamla hung around should the woman call again. She didn't.

She was driving to another pay phone.

৪৩

His desperation and empathy with the woman prompted Hari Dixit to be patient and put his best foot forward. So, he:

- Confirmed his father's name, spouse's name, full postal address, retirement date, EPIC number.
- Confirmed his possession of the CD, offered to share the details of what he had seen *if needed, though I wouldn't like to enter into that sort of conversation with someone the age of my daughter-in-law.*
- Assured her that he wanted only – and only – information in return; any information on Varun, a clear answer to whether he had been blackmailing her.
- Reasoned patiently with her skepticism around not being returned the CD after she answered his questions.

Madam, I understand your position. Look at it this way. You have something I need. I have something you need. We will need to trust each other.

Then:

You are worried about the CD falling into the wrong hands again? But think. Why would I do that? I have as many good reasons to keep it secret as you have. If it comes to light, there will only be embarrassment for my family, people spitting at the memory of my dead son.

- Lied about not retaining a copy of the CD, though he had every intention to take it to the police if the investigation merited it.

Somewhere, we will need to believe each other. I will believe...have no choice but to believe what you say. You will believe – have, I think, little choice but to believe – that I will return your property, not bother you again after I have the information I need. That's the only way we both get what we want.

Then:

You are worried about the CD being misused. But who in his right mind wants to sully the memory of his late son, risk family disgrace?

As per the agreement reached:

- Minna Kumar would be returned the CD not by post or courier (it may get lost/ the receiving address would be revealed/ the package may be received by someone else at home) but personally. She would be in India for a cousin's wedding in Delhi in mid-March and a suitable date, time and place would be agreed for the handover. Till then, Hari Dixit would keep the CD safe.
- Only one of Hari Dixit's questions would be answered now. All others would have to wait till the CD was handed over.

Later, Minna felt the terms of the agreement were skewed against her, felt that she had been swayed by the man's pitch. She consoled herself with the thought that it was the best she could have negotiated in her situation. It hadn't occurred to her to ask how Varun had died. Should she have asked, as a courtesy perhaps?

To Hari Dixit, Minna Kumar's lack of interest in how and why Varun died suggested not lack of courtesy, but lack of guilt. When he entered the Vikrant Vihar Police Station at the appointed hour, it was with the unsettling knowledge that his son had been a blackmailer.

ॐ

The Platinum Heights complex was off the road, surrounded by more than a dozen construction sites and little else. The nearest populated complex was a kilometer away. The only business establishments around were property dealers' offices, a few tea-cigarette stalls. No taxi stands.

C Block, their specific destination, was the only complete block in the complex; it's entrance lobby a mess, lift untidy but functional. Clotheslines and air conditioners outside, nameplates in the lobby suggested that only about six or seven of the forty-odd flats in the block were occupied.

The two other blocks in the complex stood unfinished. Dirty white flags carrying the builder's logo fluttered sadly in surrender to market or court diktats. Only those could halt real estate activity so effectively in Gurgaon.

The apartment itself was poorly furnished.

Drawing room: No TV; readymade curtains; furniture that looked old, possibly second-hand.

Kitchen: A few basic utensils strewn; one complete set of plates, serving bowls and cutlery; an old looking, near empty fridge but for an unopened carton of orange juice, an unopened packet of bread, some eggs, a new packet of butter; more cooking ingredients on the slab than inside cupboards; nothing unwashed in the sink.

Only one of the two bedrooms appeared to have been in use. Inside it: a bed; no TV; readymade curtains; a half-full cupboard of clothes, footwear, cosmetics, a chest of drawers with some fraying undergarments and socks; no jewelry.

In the attached bathroom: recently opened bar of soap, a near full bottle of shampoo, some creams, new looking toothbrush, toothpaste, some shaving razors.

In the designated parking slot: No car.

Of the families that occupied the building, two identified Leena Puri from the picture.

Family # 1: She came one afternoon asking for milk. We were out of stock ourselves having returned earlier the same day from an outstation wedding. *You would be able to pinpoint the date then?* I'll have to check with my mother-in-law. She has a habit of hoarding wedding invitation cards. One minute. Yes, here. The wedding was on 19th November, so it was the 20th of November when she came. *Anything you can recall about her that day?* There was this big silver ring that covered almost her entire thumb. Clearly visible because of the way she held the glass. *Anything else?* No, nothing else that stood out. The ring did for size, the finger on which it was worn.

Family # 2: She came one afternoon asking for milk. We gave it. *Remember the date?* Not exactly but it wasn't too long ago. *About five-six weeks ago? Around 20th November, you would say?* That seems about right. *Anything you can recall about her that day?* There was this big silver ring that covered almost her entire thumb. Clearly visible because of the way she held the glass. *Anything else?* No, nothing else that stood out. The ring did for size, the finger on which it was worn.

On the way back, they discussed what they had seen.

- Agreed that there had been something peculiar about Leena Puri.

- Agreed on the need to find more about Leena Puri from Bindia Sehgal.
- Hoped there would be something helpful in the unmarked CD found on the bed.

Who keeps a CD without a TV, CD player or computer at home, the Inspector wondered aloud. Did she get hold of the CD by murdering Varun, Hari Dixit wondered silently. He already had an idea of what was on it.

Bindia Sehgal offered to come to the station. The old man offered to keep away but had a few 'suggestions' on what to ask her. They turned out to be rather useful suggestions.

৪১

[Scene: SHO Ajai Singh's Office, Vikrant Vihar Police Station.]

[The Inspector and Bindia Sehgal are talking. Bindia Sehgal clearly hasn't forgotten her first meeting with Ajai Singh and is either curt or irritated for the most part. Her demeanor suggests that she finds Ajai Singh's questions repetitive and pointless.]

Ajai Singh: We noticed a few things at Platinum Heights, madam, and wanted to discuss them with you.

Bindia Sehgal: Three weeks have passed.

Ajai Singh: I was told you called a few times. Unfortunately, there was nothing concrete to share.

Bindia Sehgal: Last time I was told there was a lead. Before that I was told of plans to get call records.

Ajai Singh: The CDRs should come soon.

Bindia Sehgal: What about the leads?

Ajai Singh: They are there. That's why we went to Platinum Heights.

Bindia Sehgal: Okay.

Ajai Singh: Leenaji had…has…a rather withdrawn existence?

Bindia Sehgal: She's always been moody. Ever since school.

Ajai Singh: Still, it is strange. No TV, Internet, newspaper at home. Little contact with neighbors. No help to cook, clean.

Bindia Sehgal: No help? Really?

Ajai Singh: We spoke to a few maids who work in the complex. None of them had been in her employ or knew anybody else who had been.

Bindia Sehgal: That's strange. Not engaging a full-timer, I understand. We don't have one ourselves – find it unnecessary after my son left for boarding and husband started traveling more after taking up a new job – but no help at all is strange, tough.

Ajai Singh: It's not only a question of not having help at home.

Bindia Sehgal: I can believe Leena wanting to keep a distance from neighbors. We re-connected after more than twenty-five years and I got the sense she wanted to be left alone.

Ajai Singh nods.

Bindia Sehgal: I offered to introduce her to friends, suggested joining Facebook, WhatsApp, invited her to gatherings. She wasn't interested. The prospect of human contact seems to hassle her.

Ajai Singh: Any particular reason why she wanted…wants… to keep to herself?

Bindia Sehgal: No. She says nothing – and that's why I believe she wants to be left alone. She avoids discussing what happened during the time we were out of touch.

Ajai Singh: You have no idea of her life in America?

Bindia Sehgal: No, but whatever happened was not good.

Ajai Singh: Why do you say that?

Bindia Sehgal: When she turned up, she said she had nowhere to go, no money, no job. I have rarely seen anyone that sad.

Ajai Singh: This was when?

Bindia Sehgal: About three-four months ago.

Ajai Singh: Can you be more specific?

Bindia Sehgal: Mid, maybe end, September.

Ajai Singh: So one September day she suddenly appeared at your doorstep?

Bindia Sehgal: Not exactly my doorstep.

Ajai Singh: Then?

Bindia Sehgal: She called one morning, said she was in town, wanted to meet up. We met at a coffee shop.

Ajai Singh: She called on your mobile.

Bindia Sehgal: Yes.

Ajai Singh: From landline?

Bindia Sehgal: No, mobile.

Ajai Singh: The same number she called you on the date of her disappearance?

Bindia Sehgal: Yes.

Ajai Singh: That's the only mobile number she had?

Bindia Sehgal: It's the only mobile number she's called me from.

Ajai Singh: How did Leenaji find you after so many years?

Bindia Sehgal: I don't know.

Ajai Singh: You didn't ask? It's a natural thing to ask someone who reconnects after a long time.

Bindia Sehgal: I might have asked, she might have replied, I don't remember. We are talking of a conversation that happened months ago. Moreover, she was looking depressed. My focus wasn't on finding how she found me.

Ajai Singh: So you have no idea how she found you?

Bindia Sehgal: No idea.

Ajai Singh: Hmm.

Bindia Sehgal: If you want me to guess, I would say it was over the net.

Ajai Singh: Internet? From what little I know, it would've been difficult.

Bindia Sehgal: Actually, it's the easiest way to find someone these days.

Ajai Singh: I don't know if that applies here. There would be several people with the same name as yours. Pictures wouldn't have helped either. Also, there was no guarantee you were in Delhi-NCR.

Bindia Sehgal: Right.

Ajai Singh: Could she have found you via a common acquaintance?

Bindia Sehgal: I don't think so. I'm pretty sure Leena isn't in touch with any of the school gang.

Ajai Singh: Any common acquaintances other than school people?

Bindia Sehgal: None from the past. And after return, like I said, she refused my offer to introduce her to any of my friends.

Ajai Singh: Jog your memory a bit, madam. If there was someone through whom she found you, that someone may be able to tell us something useful. She could be in touch with that person right now as we speak.

Bindia Sehgal (after some reflection): I think…not a hundred percent confirmed…but I think…she said it was the school alumna website where she found me. My mobile number is there.

Ajai Singh: At school, you wouldn't have been Bindia Sehgal?

Bindia Sehgal: Meaning?

Ajai Singh: You would have had another surname in school. The Sehgal title came post-marriage, right? So, how did Leenaji know it was the right Bindia she was contacting?

Bindia Sehgal: Oh. Okay. I was the only Bindia around our time in school.

Ajai Singh: The school list mentions your batch year?

Bindia Sehgal: My batch details are there because I was elected to one of the Alumna Association Committees recently.

Ajai Singh: It would also have details of others you both were in school with?

Bindia Sehgal: Not everybody. For others' details, one needs to register on the site or call the association office. Only office bearers' details are public view.

Ajai Singh: So, you were the easiest school-time friend to find?

Bindia Sehgal: That's one way to look at it. I like to think Leena would have sought me out before anyone else.

Ajai Singh: Of course, of course. You were close. Leenaji is registered on the school site?

Bindia Sehgal: I suggested, but she wasn't interested. Before you ask if she could have registered without my knowledge, the answer is no. We get a mail notification when someone registers.

Ajai Singh (smiles): You didn't have a problem recognizing her after such a long gap?

Bindia Sehgal: If she had passed me by on the street, I don't know whether I would have. Seeing her before me, knowing it was Leena I was seeing, made it easier I guess.

Ajai Singh: I wouldn't recognize someone I last saw in school.

Bindia Sehgal: She recollected conversations that had happened exclusively between us, stories we had shared with no one else. We were close. There are things only we know about each other.

Ajai Singh: It couldn't have been someone trying to pass off as Leena Puri then?

Bindia Sehgal: Of course not.

Ajai Singh: How did she recognize you?

Bindia Sehgal: My picture's on the Alumna Association site.

Ajai Singh: Do understand, madam. It's my job to ask questions. Some of them may seem rude or irrelevant and I'll request your indulgence. Impatience will not help the investigation.

Bindia Sehgal: Fine.

Ajai Singh: She had come from America?

Bindia Sehgal: That's what she said.

Ajai Singh: Contacted you from the airport?

Bindia Sehgal: I don't think. She mentioned staying at a lodge for a few days. I remember because she said it was real shady.

Ajai Singh: Did she mention the name of the lodge or where it was?

Bindia Sehgal: Only that it was shady.

Ajai Singh: Can you recall the exact date you met?

Bindia Sehgal: It was mid, maybe end, September.

Ajai Singh: You said that before. An approximate date at least?

Bindia Sehgal: Won't call data help with that? There will be calls between us from around the date we met.

Ajai Singh: Right-right. So, would you say she returned to India sometime in the first half of September? I'm back calculating. You said she contacted you in the second half of September and had stayed in a lodge for a few days before that.

Bindia Sehgal: The way you say it, first half September seems right. Maybe a few days here and there.

Ajai Singh: That's all right. I am trying to get a rough window. The passport people may be able to dig out something once we provide them a window.

Bindia Sehgal (after a pause): If you are asking for such a specific reason, I will have to admit I'm unsure. Sorry.

Ajai Singh: Why?

Bindia Sehgal: Thinking back, I recall she said she had returned from the US recently. How recently, I don't know. She didn't say.

Ajai Singh: Nevertheless, you are saying it wasn't very long after America return that she contacted you.

Bindia Sehgal: Yes.

Ajai Singh: You are also saying she was in a lodge for at least some part of the period between her return and contacting you.

Bindia Sehgal nods.

Ajai Singh: The only thing you are uncertain about is whether she stayed for a while in some other place before the lodge.

Bindia Sehgal: Yes.

Ajai Singh: And you have no idea where that other place would be?

Bindia Sehgal: No. She could well have checked into the lodge on the day she arrived. Or could have stayed in some decent place before running out of money and moving into the lodge. I don't know.

Ajai Singh: Hmm.

Bindia Sehgal: You do realize that these questions sound relevant in retrospect, but aren't the sort one dwells on when one meets a friend after many years?

Ajai Singh: Especially if the friend doesn't seem in good condition. I get that.

Bindia Sehgal (wondering if the cop is being sarcastic): Right.

Ajai Singh: Finally, you are saying you have no idea if she met anyone else between the time she returned and the time she contacted you.

Bindia Sehgal: No, no idea.

Ajai Singh: Okay.

[Ajai Singh pauses to think of his next line of enquiry.
Bindia Sehgal looks around with a bored expression.]

Ajai Singh: When Leenaji turned up...turned up...the way you say she did, did she say what she wanted from you? Specifically?

Bindia Sehgal: Nothing explicitly but it was clear she wanted help, was too proud to ask. I asked her what brought her to town, where she was planning to go, what she was planning to do, she kept saying I don't know, I don't know.

Ajai Singh: What about relatives?

Bindia Sehgal: Leena's an only child. Her mother passed away when she was very young. Contact broke with the mother's side of the family after that. It was with her father that she went to the US. That was in Class VIII. She mentioned he passed away too.

Ajai Singh: Okay.

Bindia Sehgal: I also know that her dada and dadi are no more. There was an aunt too. Uncle's sister. I don't remember her name, have no idea where she is now.

Ajai Singh: Marriage? Children?

Bindia Sehgal: I told you before. If Leena married, it didn't seem to have ended well. I might be wrong, but the sense I got is that she never married.

Ajai Singh: Then you decided to help?

Bindia Sehgal: Yes. Offered our empty flat at Platinum Heights, gave her some money to set it up.

Ajai Singh: Been to the flat recently?

Bindia Sehgal: Not in a while. But I know it isn't a great place to live.

Ajai Singh: Leenaji didn't...doesn't...have a car? The parking slot doesn't seem used.

Bindia Sehgal: No. She uses taxis generally.

Ajai Singh: There are no taxi stands near Platinum Heights.

Bindia Sehgal: I offer to drop her home whenever we meet but she always declines, says she'll take a taxi. So, I assume she uses taxis. Could be booking online.

Ajai Singh: Always uses taxis? Platinum Heights isn't far from your residence. On the other side of the main road, not in a settled residential zone, but not far distance-wise. Not more than two kilometers.

Bindia Sehgal: True. Sometimes she said she had to go somewhere else. Sometimes she said dropping would only delay me. I did not insist.

Ajai Singh: How does she get by, manage her expenses?

Bindia Sehgal: I lent some money.

Ajai Singh: A second time, after the money for setting-up?

Bindia Sehgal: Yes. She was reluctant to accept. I told her to treat it as a loan, pay once her reiki practice took off.

Ajai Singh: Reiki practice?

Bindia Sehgal: She's thinking of starting one. You know reiki?

Ajai Singh (smiles at the snobbery): Thanks to a bad back. She did a reiki course? Here?

Bindia Sehgal: Back in the US.

Ajai Singh: Where is she planning to start?

Bindia Sehgal: In Gurgaon itself. The plan's in early stage. No specific space has been found if that's what you wanted to know. I guess she wants to get on with life.

Ajai Singh: She would have spoken to property dealers, pamphlet printers.

Bindia Sehgal: Not that I know of.

Ajai Singh: Three months is sufficient time to start off.

Bindia Sehgal shrugs.

Ajai Singh: Leenaji had gone underground a few times before.

Bindia Sehgal nods.

Ajai Singh: Where did she go?

Bindia Sehgal: The first time she went missing, I asked her. She said she had gone for some naturopathy thing at Rai. Gandhi Ashram something something.

Ajai Singh: Rai? Sonepat?

Bindia Sehgal (nods): I checked their website out of curiosity. It was quite affordable, so I could believe. But then I called the center and they said they hadn't had anyone of her name or description.

Ajai Singh: You told this to Leenaji?

Bindia Sehgal: I made the mistake.

Ajai Singh: Mistake?

Bindia Sehgal: She was very upset, said where she had been was none of my business, threatened to go away forever if I pried again.

Ajai Singh nods.

Bindia Sehgal: After cooling down a bit, she said she needed space to heal, that I need not worry if she wasn't reachable sometimes.

Ajai Singh: You stopped trying to trace her when she went underground after that?

Bindia Sehgal: It's what she wanted.

Ajai Singh: Any person – friend, acquaintance – she mentioned in recent times? People from her past, not necessarily people you may have known?

Bindia Sehgal: No. She never speaks of anybody.

Ajai Singh: Nor do you pry.

Bindia Sehgal (with a near sigh): Nor do I pry.

Ajai Singh: You are close, supporting her in many ways if I may say so. Yet, she didn't disclose anything, you didn't ask at any point?

Bindia Sehgal: Look, you need to understand what kind of person she is. Living in my house, taking money from me would be hurting her pride. I have no intention to add to her misery by using leverage I have to ask uncomfortable questions. Certainly not leverage I have because of money lent.

Ajai Singh: That last call of hers?

Bindia Sehgal: What about it?

Ajai Singh: Any idea what matter she could have been referring to? Where she could have been going? Who she was planning to meet?

Bindia Sehgal: No idea.

Ajai Singh: It would have surprised you?

Bindia Sehgal: What?

Ajai Singh: That she was going to meet someone? That there was something important she hadn't shared with you?

Bindia Sehgal: We have been through this before.

Ajai Singh (waits till he realizes Bindia Sehgal isn't going to add more): Has the name Varun Dixit come up in your conversations?

Bindia Sehgal: No.

Ajai Singh: Sure?

Bindia Sehgal: Yes. Why?

Ajai Singh: She met one Varun Dixit at about 9.30 p.m. on 16thDecember.

Bindia Sehgal: That was after her last call to me.

Ajai Singh: They were seen together at a club in Delhi.

Bindia Sehgal: That's a...surprise. Her meeting someone at a club. You positive it was Leena?

Ajai Singh: The CCTV footage from the club matches the picture you gave us.

Bindia Sehgal: Can't this Dixit tell you more?

Ajai Singh: Varun Dixit is dead, madam. He was murdered in his own flat the next day. Leenaji was...is...among the last people he was seen with.

Bindia Sehgal: Oh.

Ajai Singh: We see a link between the two cases.

Bindia Sehgal: I can tell you something with full confidence, Inspector Singh. Because I think I now have a good idea of how your department thinks. Leena may be strange, Leena may be moody, but she isn't capable of murder.

Ajai Singh: We aren't saying that either. Not at this point.

Bindia Sehgal: But you are saying the man is dead and Leena, who he was seen with a day before, is missing. I am just putting your two points together.

Ajai Singh: What time did you meet Leenaji on the 16th?

Bindia Sehgal: Around 11 a.m. Some of the shops were still opening. We parted around 1.30 p.m.

Ajai Singh: She came from home?

Bindia Sehgal: I would think so. Where else would she be coming from?

Ajai Singh: You think there's nothing odd about two Gurgaon residents living close to each other reaching Hauz Khas Village separately?

Bindia Sehgal: It's odd, yes. But it was our established pattern. She used her transport. I used mine.

Ajai Singh: Does Leenaji have a large ring that covers almost her entire thumb?

Bindia Sehgal (thinks before replying): Yes, she does. Why?

Ajai Singh: The two neighbors who have seen her remember the ring.

Bindia Sehgal: It is a standout piece.

Ajai Singh: She wasn't wearing the ring in the CCTV footage we have of the 16th.

Bindia Sehgal: It's not a piece she wears all the time.

Ajai Singh: We didn't see the ring in Platinum Heights. Nor for that matter any other jewelry.

Bindia Sehgal: So?

Ajai Singh (ignoring the question, clearly building up to something): There was no suitcase at Platinum Heights either. When she came to you, she had a suitcase?

Bindia Sehgal: Yes.

Ajai Singh: There is no jewelry or suitcase in the flat. Neither are the clothes that she was seen wearing that day. Nor the clothes you reported seeing her last in, or those she is seen wearing in the CCTV footage.

Bindia Sehgal (rubs her forehead): Sorry. This is getting confusing for me. What are you trying to say?

Ajai Singh: Leenaji left home on the morning of 16th December with a suitcase, some clothes and whatever jewelry she may have had.

Bindia Sehgal: I would've noticed a suitcase.

Ajai Singh: She could've left it in the vehicle she was using. Or she left home before the 16th.

Bindia Sehgal: Maybe, I don't know. But if she left before the 16th, you mean to say she didn't spend 15th night at home? That's…strange.

Ajai Singh: It is safe to say she didn't spend 16th night there and carried a suitcase, jewelry and some clothes before leaving home. Either on 16th morning or earlier.

Bindia Sehgal (finally getting the Inspector's point): You are saying that…that…her disappearance was planned?

Ajai Singh: Looks like that, won't you say?

Bindia Sehgal: She's gone missing before, but not this long. That's what worries me.

Ajai Singh: That worries us too. Plus, the fact that she met Varun Dixit a night before his murder and has been missing from around that time…

Bindia Sehgal: …is the reason you are saying…the two cases are linked.

Ajai Singh nods.

Bindia Sehgal: I know her better than any living person, Inspector Singh, and I will say it again. She isn't capable of murder.

Ajai Singh: We are not saying she's a suspect.

Bindia Sehgal (exasperated): Anyway, my questions remain. Where is Leena? Is she safe? How long will you take to find her?

Ajai Singh: We can't rule out the worst. However, if it's any consolation, you should know there's nothing yet to show the worst has occurred.

Bindia Sehgal (turning emotional): I hope she's safe. We are very close, Inspector. Like sisters.

Ajai Singh (in a softer tone): We're doing our best, madam.

Bindia Sehgal (gathering herself): What happens next?

Ajai Singh: We keep looking for Leenaji. Her and Varun Dixit's CDRs should be coming today. There's no reason to give up.

Bindia Sehgal: On that somewhat hopeful note, Inspector, one request...unless there's any other point you wanted to discuss...

Ajai Singh: No. Go on. Please.

Bindia Sehgal: I was helping Leena without my husband's knowledge. He doesn't know about her stay at Platinum Heights or the money I passed. If you can keep that information to yourselves...

Ajai Singh: That is why you chose to drop and pick the keys here.

Bindia Sehgal nods.

Ajai Singh: Okay. We will maintain silence for now. Do know though that the information will be held back only till it can be held back. If the investigation takes a turn where we need to disclose it to others, we will.

Bindia Sehgal: That's fine. I hope to tell my husband on Saturday. You can hold on till then?

Ajai Singh: Saturday?

Bindia Sehgal: Ashok, Mr Sehgal, is generally in Mumbai during the week on work, returns for weekends. I did not move because I am comfortable here, can't bring myself to leave Gurgaon. Mumbai scares me.

Ajai Singh: Till Saturday should be fine. I did not want to give a false assurance.

Bindia Sehgal: No, no, that's absolutely fine. Anything else?

Ajai Singh: We might bother you again if other questions come up.

Bindia Sehgal: No problem. I'll get going then.

[Bindia Sehgal leaves. Ajai Singh half rises, buzzes a constable, lets out an audible sigh once Bindia Sehgal is out of earshot.]

৩

Hariji couldn't sleep.

Where, when had they gone wrong with Varun?

When they bought a color TV the very day he protested about having to watch matches in others' homes?

When they lied to the class teacher about having signed the diary complaints?

When they saw him posing before the mirror and said he was Amitabh Bachchan?

When they stopped insisting he wear Tarun's clothes?

When they ignored the missing film pages from magazines?

When they settled the school canteen dues without question?

Where, when had they failed Varun?

Where, when had they failed themselves?

৩

Hari Dixit still couldn't sleep.

The Inspector deserved an apology for keeping the Minna Kumar episode secret.

What to say?

Would the Inspector remain the same after the disclosure?

Or would his father's mistaken call fail Varun again?

[Scene: SHO Ajai Singh's Office, Vikrant Vihar Police Station.]

[The Inspector is down with a cold. He coughs repeatedly into a handkerchief, examines the handkerchief and sniffles before noticing Hari Dixit at the door.]

Hari Dixit: Come in, Inspector saab?

    Ajai Singh: Yes-yes. How come early morning today? Sit.

    Hari Dixit: There was something important I wanted to tell.

    Ajai Singh: Tell.

    Hari Dixit: Actually I am here to apologize.

    Ajai Singh: Apologize? For what?

    Hari Dixit (softly): Keeping you in the dark about something. The guilt's been eating me, keeping me awake.

    Ajai Singh gives a perplexed look.

    Hari Dixit: I kept something hidden from you, shouldn't have done that. Not after your kindnesses.

    Ajai Singh: Come on. What's so serious that merits such a preamble?

    Hari Dixit: I...uh...I...

    Ajai Singh: Now you are only increasing suspense.

Hari Dixit: After returning from Lucknow, I got Varun's bank locker opened, found two CDs there.

Ajai Singh: Okay?

Hari Dixit: Both CDs showed the same thing. A woman in a compromising position. There was a mobile number mentioned on the CD cover. The number is with someone else now. Through the current holder I found the contact details of the person who was holding it at the time the video was made.

Ajai Singh: Okay.

Hari Dixit: Her name is Minna Kumar, she lives in Australia and confirmed Varun was blackmailing her.

Ajai Singh arches his brows.

Hari Dixit: I beg your forgiveness, Inspector saab. I should've told you earlier. I kept quiet because I wanted to protect my son's dignity in death. Also the woman in the video. I promised to keep it safe.

[Awkward silence.]

Ajai Singh: The woman could be behind the murder.

Hari Dixit (hesitantly): Doesn't seem like that. I did not disclose how Varun died and she never asked. If she were guilty, she would've tried to get some information.

Ajai Singh: Did she say anything else?

Hari Dixit: Nothing much. She only confirmed blackmail, says she will answer any other question only after she gets the CD back.

Ajai Singh: How do you know she's not in India?

Hari Dixit: The woman who passed on her contact details told me she was in Australia. The number she called me from was Australian. Also she says she can collect the CD only in

March, not before. If she were in the country, she would've tried to get hold of it earlier.

Ajai Singh: True.

[Another awkward silence.]

Ajai Singh: You are telling me now because of the CD we found yesterday? You think it's a similar CD, a CD made for black... for a similar purpose?

Hari Dixit (with downcast eyes): I am sorry, Inspector saab.

Ajai Singh: Enough. You are my senior. No matter. Let bygones be bygones. In the future, let us be open with each other.

Hari Dixit (looking up, avoiding the Inspector's eyes): There will be no cause for complaint ever again. I guarantee.

Ajai Singh: Shall we close the chapter now? We will see the CD tomorrow when the operator comes. Let's see what it has. Unless you know how to see it?

Hari Dixit: I learnt recently.

Ajai Singh: Let's watch now then.

Hari Dixit (brings out a CD from inside his jacket): Someone here can switch on the computer?

Ajai Singh: The Station Clerk can manage.

[Ajai Singh buzzes the Station Clerk.
A sheepish Hari Dixit fiddles with the CD.]

Ajai Singh: The CDRs came yesterday.

Hari Dixit: Anything coming out?

Ajai Singh: Several things. Inspector Bakshi had to explain. People like me would have drowned in the details otherwise.

Hari Dixit: What does Bakshi saab say?

[Station Clerk enters.]

Ajai Singh: Let's finish with the videos first.

[Ajai Singh says something to the Station Clerk. Ajai Singh and Hari Dixit watch the Station Clerk switch on the computer.]

౷

They watched the video twice. Leena Puri frolicked on a bed. The location looked like a hotel room but the camera angle and lighting offered no clues on which hotel it was. Then they saw the video with Minna Kumar. Though there was a difference in how the women came across (Minna Kumar inert as if drugged; Leena Puri in a top and skirt, smiling, teasing, deliberately provocative – bending to show cleavage, wriggling buttocks, running her hands down her stomach, raising dress to reveal thigh), the intent behind the filming was not.

Neither man remembered seeing the top and skirt at Platinum Heights.

౷

WHAT THE CDRs SAID		
Item	**Varun Dixit**	**Leena Puri**
Service Provider	WiWorld	iWish
Type of Connection	Post-paid	Pre-paid
Date of Activation	14 March 2011	19 December 2013[1]
Usage Pattern	Normal	Erratic; few calls, long switch-off periods
Most Frequently Called Numbers	Lucknow landline number[2]; a Western UP Telecom Circle mobile number[3]; 3-4 Delhi Metro Telecom Circle mobile numbers[4]	Only three individuals called: Varun Dixit[5]; Bindia Sehgal[6]; a Delhi Metro Telecom Circle mobile number (five times, all in February 2014)
Time, Date and Probable Location of Switch-off	3.24 p.m., 17 December 2014[7]; probable location: Varun Dixit residence	9.39 p.m., 16 December 2014[8]; probable location: within 2 km radius of Leena Puri residence[9]
Last Call Before Switch-off	Incoming call at 2.32 p.m., 17 December 2014 from Lucknow landline number[10]	Outgoing call to Bindia Sehgal at 8.13 p.m. on 16 December 2014[11]
Calls 24 hours Prior to Switch-off (other than last call above)	Incoming call from Leena Puri at 1.37 p.m. on 16 December 2014 (probable location: Hauz Khas Village)[12] One outgoing (unanswered) call to Leena Puri at 9.15 p.m. of 16 December 2014 (probable location: Spiff) Four other calls (two incoming, two outgoing), all from/ to separate Delhi Metro Telecom Circle mobile numbers[13]	Outgoing call to Varun Dixit at 1.37 p.m. on 16 December 2014 One incoming (unanswered) call from Varun Dixit at 9.15 p.m. of 16 December 2014

WHAT THE CDRs SAID		
Item	**Varun Dixit**	**Leena Puri**
Notable Calls Received After Switch-off	Two calls from a Western UP Telecom Circle mobile number at 7.08 p.m. and 7.47 p.m. of 17 December 2014[14] Eight calls from Hari Dixit's mobile – six on 18 December 2014 and two on 19 December 2014 Two calls from one of the four recently spoken to Delhi Metro Telecom Circle mobile number subscribers	Over a dozen calls from Bindia Sehgal including one at 10.34 p.m. of 16 December 2014[15]
Subscriber Name and Address	Varun Dixit, A- 403, Pride Apartments, Vikrant Vihar-II, Gurgaon 122 013	Ratan Lal, H. No. 454, Pole No. 483, Sanjay Colony, Thijwasan, Delhi 110 061[16]

Notes: (1) Leena Puri returned to India much before she contacted Bindia Sehgal? (2) Dixit residence. (3) Hari Dixit. (4) Probably friends or business associates. (5) Long, frequent calls up to end-March 2014; reduced contact after that. First call post-activation was made to Varun Dixit. (6) After 18 September 2014. (7) Fitting the estimated window for time of death. (8) Within minutes of exiting Spiff. (9) She had exited Spiff minutes ago. How was the phone in Gurgaon? (10) Hari Dixit had called to check after hearing of bomb threat on TV. (11) Tallying with Bindia Sehgal's report. (12) Call made soon after parting ways from Bindia Sehgal; according to Bindia Sehgal, they had parted ways around 1.30 p.m. (13) Worth checking? (14) Tarun Dixit. (15) Tallying with Bindia Sehgal's report. (16) Who the hell was Ratan Lal?

৪৩

[Scene: SHO Ajai Singh's Office, Vikrant Vihar Police Station.]

[The Inspector and Hari Dixit are in conversation. Ajai Singh continues to sneeze, sniffle.]

Ajai Singh: What's in the video is in the video. As far as the CDRs are concerned...

Hari Dixit: Ji.

Ajai Singh (changing tack): What do you make of things, Dixitji?

Hari Dixit (cautiously): Leena Puri seems a...twisted character. She lied to Bindia Sehgal about her return, was using a phone registered under someone else's name.

Ajai Singh: We also know she knew Varun Dixit for over a year, have reason to believe relations between them deteriorated following blackmail.

Hari Dixit: Given the reduced frequency of contact.

Ajai Singh: Yes. Also, her disappearance was planned.

Hari Dixit: Ji.

Ajai Singh: On top of everything, she had possession of the CD with which she was being blackmailed. It would've been taken from Pride Apartments. I say we have a suspect.

Hari Dixit nods without conviction.

Ajai Singh (misreading the nod): Sedating doesn't seem above someone who arranged a phone under a false name and lied to her sister-like friend.

Hari Dixit (hesitating): All true but...

Ajai Singh: But?

Hari Dixit: A few things jar, Inspector saab.

Ajai Singh: Like?

Hari Dixit: If it was so important to her, why didn't she take the CD?

Ajai Singh (mildly dismissive): Could have forgotten in the rush of packing.

Hari Dixit: Why did she return to Varun after getting hold of the CD?

Ajai Singh (confused): What?

Hari Dixit: Varun expired on 17th afternoon. Leena Puri hasn't returned to her flat after the 16th.

Ajai Singh: Correct.

Hari Dixit: Which means the CD would have been with her on the 16th.

Ajai Singh: Ah, I see now. It doesn't make sense to go to Pride Apartments on the 17th after she had the CD on the 16th.

Hari Dixit: Or earlier.

Ajai Singh: Or earlier. Unless the murder decision was an afterthought, something she decided to do to close matters once and for all. Which are the words she used with Bindia Sehgal.

Hari Dixit: That's likely. But why meet up on 16th night then?

Ajai Singh: To make a final payment in lieu of the CD?

Hari Dixit: That would explain the short meeting. But why go all the way to Delhi to make the final payment? They were both in Gurgaon. And why exchange money in a public place?

Ajai Singh: Maybe they were both in Delhi for some other work, found it convenient to meet there. Maybe she was getting money from somewhere in Delhi.

Hari Dixit: Why exchange money in a club?

Ajai Singh (after some thinking): Can't think of any good reason.

Hari Dixit: More than that, why pay after already getting hold of the CD?

Ajai Singh: She was baiting him for murder that night but something happened, something to postpone the plan?

Hari Dixit: Could be.

[Silence as the duo think.]

Ajai Singh: Okay, my turn to poke holes. Assuming Leena Puri forgot the CD, she had time to pick it. Why didn't she?

Hari Dixit: Perhaps she didn't realize she had left it in the flat.

Ajai Singh: Could she – mistakenly – have thought she was carrying it? Though it's difficult to believe why someone would forget the very thing they killed for.

Hari Dixit: That's not the only forgetful thing she did. She forgot her phone in Gurgaon. The last call was from Gurgaon at around 8.15 p.m., the phone was in Gurgaon when it was switched off at 9.39 p.m. Leena Puri was in Delhi around that time.

Ajai Singh: Strange. She plans her disappearance carefully, remembers to pack jewelry and clothes, but forgets the CD and her phone.

Hari Dixit: Could she have dropped the phone somewhere? Somebody would have found it, thrown the SIM, pocketed the instrument.

Ajai Singh: Sounds unlikely.

Hari Dixit: Do you think someone could have picked and destroyed it on her instruction?

Ajai Singh: That someone can be Bindia Sehgal. But Bindia Sehgal, as far as we know, was at home. There's no way of establishing she left home that night.

Hari Dixit: True. They don't have a maid at home, the husband was traveling, the driver would have left for the day and security folk wouldn't keep record of a resident going and coming in.

Ajai Singh: Anyway, it couldn't have been Bindia Sehgal. If she was being sent to pick Leena Puri's phone, why not ask her to clear the CD too?

Hari Dixit: That's also there.

Ajai Singh: Let's leave this line at the moment. We are going around in circles. Come to some fundamental questions.

Hari Dixit: Ji.

Ajai Singh: Why blackmail Leena Puri? She didn't have much money.

Hari Dixit: Maybe that's why an early settlement was reached.

Ajai Singh: Phone contact reduced between them after March. That would have been when the blackmail began? Roughly nine-ten months after the two met? That doesn't suggest early settlement.

Hari Dixit nods.

Ajai Singh: Moreover, the video itself is not as…as…damning as Minna Kumar's. At one level, it's just a woman dancing. Like a bar dancer or something.

Hari Dixit: She is clearly doing it for a single-person audience though. What the video would suggest to an outside person is that the woman is intimate with the person filming her, free enough with the person filming her to do…much…more with him. Though we don't get to see what happens, there's a feeling something follows.

Ajai Singh: Right. That element of comfort between the two, the suggestion of something more, something wrong that is likely to follow or actually followed, is what a blackmailer would cash on.

Hari Dixit: Ji.

Ajai Singh: But why would someone like Leena Puri be afraid of blackmail, especially blackmail over a dance video like this? It's not as if she had any family to face.

Hari Dixit: Another puzzle.

Ajai Singh: There's no circumstantial evidence either. Nothing to confirm Leena Puri was inside or near Pride Apartments at the time of murder. How did she enter the Pride Apartments complex?

Hari Dixit: We could visit the complex again, show her picture around. It may ring a bell.

Ajai Singh: Maybe.

Hari Dixit: You might want to check with the resident's association when the guards who were on duty on 17th afternoon are going to be around. It'll save time.

Ajai Singh: There are a few other things to do as well. It may be worthwhile sending someone to talk to Ratan Lal and the person Leena Puri spoke to regularly in February.

[Scene fades. They continue talking inaudibly.]

WED 7 JANUARY 2015

It was exactly the sort of home Ajai Singh imagined a cult to be operating from. Chants playing in the background, silk hangings with colorful images of dragons, monkeys and Chinese boatmen, overpowering smell of incense, plentiful floor seating, posh-looking people speaking in hushed tones, thin, silver-haired host in loose clothes. But for bindi and lipstick, her husband looked no different from her.

It was the husband, a retired tobacco firm head, who spoke to them.

Yes, the fracas at the gate had been caused by one of theirs. The local chapter met every Wednesday afternoon, between 3 and 5 p.m. Around thirty people turned up every time to meditate, share experiences. None had ever been asked to make an entry at the gate before today. With new security regulations after the unfortunate occurrence – the murder the Inspector was referring to – PAWA had decided to make no exceptions in its Board Meeting of 4th January. That is what had upset one of the members. Egos were fragile these days. A priority problem the group was trying hard to address.

Yes, difficult as it was to admit, it was possible someone entered the complex the day of the murder claiming to have come for their meeting. Knowledge of the meeting time, location could be accessed by anyone. People learnt through word of mouth, came through other members. It was an open house. All were welcome.

Yes, he maintained a database of those who attended. Well, database was a fancy word. It was some basic data. Only of those who volunteered details. There was no compulsion. Just attendees' names, phone numbers, addresses. He would be happy to run through it but wasn't it likely the person never entered the meeting? Or even if she – you said it was a woman – did, she may not have shared her details or shared false details.

Of course, no harm in checking. The face in this photo isn't familiar, but then one sees so many faces. It's difficult to remember. Especially since many attend one or two meetings and opt out.

You are in luck, Inspector. There is one Leena Puri here. Platinum Heights. She's the one?

Okay. She was here on 24th December.

Yes, 24th December

No, not 17th but 24th.

Very sure. I make it a point to make entries date-wise.

We can show the picture around. Some of the regulars are here. Maybe they'll remember.

Sorry. None of them recall her.

No, there's no mistake. One Leena Puri from Platinum Heights came on 24th December.

Hope this has been helpful.

৪৩

Leena Puri drops off the radar on 16th December, attends a meeting in the complex where Varun Dixit is murdered on 24th December. She had known about the Wednesday afternoon meetings at Pride Apartments, used the knowledge to gain entry on the 17th. But why did she visit Pride Apartments again on the 24th? And why did she volunteer information, correct information? Was it someone trying to pass off as Leena Puri? Why would anyone do that? To all those questions, there were no answers.

To one question, there was (?). If it were Leena Puri who came to the meeting on the 24th, where would she have been between 16th and 24th? It couldn't have been her home. She hadn't been there since at least the 16th. In need, there was, as far as they knew, only one person in the world she could have turned to.

So:

Was Bindia Sehgal hiding her friend? If yes, where?

Then:

Why was Bindia Sehgal hiding her friend? Did she know her friend was a murderer? Had Bindia Sehgal lied about not having heard of Varun Dixit? Had she helped in Varun's murder? Had she made a missing person's complaint to throw the police off?

Then:

How did the reclusive Leena Puri come to know Varun Dixit? Through Bindia Sehgal, her lone window to the world?

ॐ

The men reported.

Ratan Lal, a car driver nearing fifty, was in his village in Bihar to settle a land dispute. Contacted over the phone via son Raju, he said he: (a) had never known, approached for work or been in the employ of a Leena Puri or any woman of her description; (b) couldn't think how a number in his name was with a madam in Gurgaon. No, nobody, male or female, had ever bought his mobile or paid him to get a connection.

Do you see reason to doubt Ratan Lal?

No, sir. He sounded genuinely surprised.

Car showroom manager, Sujit Pal, thirty-four, admitted having spoken to one Leena Puri a few times in February 2014. They met on the net, exchanged numbers, spoke on phone, chatted a few times on WhatsApp but a meeting never materialized. Conversations gradually lost spark; contact reduced, stopped.

Leena Puri had claimed to be around forty, single, living alone in Gurgaon and interested in reiki, trekking and philosophy.

He said they used WhatsApp?

Yes.

Pucca?

Sir.

Anything else of note she said that he remembered?

Nothing.

Nothing about family, work, friends?

Apparently, personal questions were off-limits. That was her Rule # 1.

Does he have chat or WhatsApp records?

No. I asked. He said he deleted it a few months ago. It was becoming an addiction, had started impacting family life. According to him, the chats were just innocent flirting. No party revealed anything substantial.

Do you see reason to doubt Sujit Pal?

No, sir. He came across as clean, frank. For him, it seemed a case of *raat gayi, baat gayi.*

৪৩

There's someone that I turn to when cases get complicated, Dixitji. If you want, we can go see him.

No-no, not a policeman. He taught us in college. Professor Kuldeep Yadav. Retired. Very wise man. Very clear thinking. He has helped me close some complicated cases. I didn't want to approach him without talking to you first.

Don't worry about that. We are close. Not that I was particularly good at his subject or anything.

I saved him from a group of agitating students once.

Daytime, he takes some civil service coaching classes. Evenings are free. There are no sons, daughters are married, and madam gets busy with cooking and TV.

I can check. We'll have to carry something though.

No, no case files. He doesn't bother with them, says he's done enough reading for a lifetime.

A bottle of McDowell No. 1. Two if we wish to keep the discussion going for long. You drink, right?

One more thing. He may come across a bit rough initially. Don't take that to heart. There's gold inside.

All right, I will speak to him about tomorrow evening. I have some other programme today.

Not my place to say this but it might be a good idea for you to return to Lucknow for a few days after meeting Professor saab. I know you haven't said anything, haven't pressed us to act urgently but the expenses involved in staying in this city are not unknown to me. There are people who need you there.

Tall, thin with short, graying hair, pencil moustache, wizened facial skin, spectacles tucked in the pocket of his crumpled white kurta, Kuldeep Yadav looked more like a Khap Panchayat leader than a retired professor. He had one simple instruction for them: Omit nothing, however trivial you may think it is. He heard them patiently, sought numerous clarifications as they went along, listed the questions occupying them.

ॐ

1. Who killed Varun Dixit?
   There was reason to suspect Leena Puri because:
   - Leena Puri and Varun Dixit knew each other. (CDRs)
   - Varun Dixit was a blackmailer. (CD recovered from Varun Dixit's bank locker; statement of Minna Kumar.)
   - Varun Dixit was blackmailing Leena Puri. (CD recovered from Platinum Heights.)
   - Leena Puri met Varun Dixit on 16th December, a day before the latter's murder. (Spiff CCTV footage; recording by Spiff guest.)
   - Leena Puri had something drastic in mind on/ around 16th December. (Statement of Bindia Sehgal.)

- Leena Puri knew of a way to get into Pride Apartments undetected. (Cult Manager's database.)
- Leena Puri gained possession of a CD that had evidence of her indiscretion. (CD recovered from Platinum Heights.)
- Leena Puri's disappearance was planned. (Missing suitcase, jewelry, clothes from Platinum Heights.)

However, questions remained:

- Why would Leena Puri succumb to blackmail?
  A typical female target for blackmail of the kind they were looking at was rich, had much to lose – face, family – if outed. Leena Puri, money-less, family-less, hardly fit the profile.
- Why would Leena Puri forget the CD?
  Leena Puri wanted to firmly put the past behind her. For that, she obtained all evidence of her indiscretion and killed Varun Dixit. If those were her motives, why leave the CD, one of the very things she had killed for? Especially since she remembered to take the laptop and phone. The realization that the laptop and phone may have additional evidence of indiscretion possibly explained why she met Varun Dixit on 16th December and met and murdered him on the 17th – after having gained possession of the CD earlier.
- Why would Leena Puri leave her phone behind on the night of the 16th? Who switched it off?
  Leena Puri planned her disappearance, left behind her phone (switched on) not far from her Gurgaon residence. Not at her residence for it would have been found there along with the CD. The phone was switched

off when she was in Delhi. Who found it, switched it
off?

- Why did Leena Puri return to Pride Apartments a
  week after the murder, then volunteer correct and self-
  incriminating details?

  Even if Leena Puri had a key, it wasn't for collecting
  something forgotten in Varun Dixit's apartment. There
  was nothing left behind to implicate her. The flat had
  been searched by the police, cleaned out by Dixitji
  subsequently.

2. Was Bindia Sehgal hiding something about:
   (a) Leena Puri's whereabouts (current; also, between 16th
   and 24th December); and,
   (b) her role in introducing Leena Puri and Varun Dixit?

It wasn't difficult to believe that:

- Bindia Sehgal knew about Leena Puri's blackmail.
- There weren't many others Leena Puri could have
  unburdened herself before.
- Leena Puri turned to Bindia Sehgal for help in planning
  and/or executing Varun Dixit's murder.
- Leena Puri turned to Bindia Sehgal for help in planning
  and/or executing her own disappearance.
- Bindia Sehgal, being the reclusive Leena Puri's lone
  window to the world, was the one most likely to have
  introduced her to Varun Dixit.

On the other hand:

- It was Bindia Sehgal who had come forward to make
  the missing person's complaint about Leena Puri. Had

Bindia Sehgal been complicit, she wouldn't have come to the police. After all, the little movement the case had seen owed to the missing person complaint.

- There was nothing in Varun Dixit's CDR to suggest that he had known Bindia Sehgal. Leena Puri had been in touch with Varun Dixit months before she re-met Bindia Sehgal.

ॐ

[Scene: Professor Yadav's drawing room. The walls are dirty yellow; the furnishing printed, predominantly brown. A few framed certificates seen on the walls. The cupboard has small trophies and family photographs. The lighting is deliberately dim; one of the two bulbs is switched on. Atop the center table: a half-finished whiskey bottle, a steel jug of water, open packets of potato chips and salted peanuts.]

[The host, Ajai Singh and Hari Dixit are seated around the center table. Hari Dixit is the least avid snacker and drinker, turns anxious every time conversation meanders. Professor Yadav tends to close his eyes when speaking.]

Kuldeep Yadav: I assume you want my take on the whole thing.

Ajai Singh: High time, Professor saab. Half the bottle's over.

Kuldeep Yadav (lifts the bottle to check, acts surprised): How did that happen?

Ajai Singh: Dixitji may be going slow, but remember there are three sinners today.

Kuldeep Yadav (places the bottle back on the table): Inspector saab, you will need to keep it flowing.

Ajai Singh: When did I say I will not, sirji? You keep your battery charged, that's all.

Kuldeep Yadav: Okay, then. At the outset, let's be clear about a few things.

Ajai Singh (looks towards Dixit): Ready?

Kuldeep Yadav: It's obvious that the two cases are linked. A known blackmailer's been murdered; the missing woman is one of his victims; they were among the last, if not the last, persons to have seen each other; and, details of the missing woman have appeared a week later in the record of a meeting held in the complex where the murder happened.

Ajai Singh: Right.

Kuldeep Yadav: Bear in mind that I am not saying the missing woman is behind the murder.

Ajai Singh: Then who is?

Kuldeep Yadav: Patience, Inspector saab, patience. We will come to that. Whoever was behind the murder, say X, knew both the woman who has disappeared and the man who was murdered. At least his address, her address, how to enter his apartment complex unchecked.

Ajai Singh: Correct.

Kuldeep Yadav: I believe X's hands wielded the knife. There was no hired help.

Ajai Singh (turning towards Dixit): The first bomb.

Hari Dixit nods.

Ajai Singh: Why do you say there was no help?

Kuldeep Yadav: X not only murdered Varun Dixit, but also spent time searching his flat. Took his laptop, phone and maybe a few other things we don't know about.

Ajai Singh: Right.

Kuldeep Yadav: There was something in the apartment, certainly in the laptop and phone, that X didn't want anyone else to get their hands on.

Ajai Singh nods.

Kuldeep Yadav: With a hired hand, there was always going to be the risk of whatever it was X wanted falling into other hands.

Ajai Singh: Also uncertainty around whether a hired hand, if sent alone, would know what to look for and search the place properly.

Kuldeep Yadav: That too.

Ajai Singh: In any case, hired hands nowadays prefer firearms.

Kuldeep Yadav: Add to all this the risk of a second person entering the apartment complex unnoticed.

Ajai Singh: Point made. What do you think, Dixitji?

Hari Dixit: I agree with Professor saab.

Ajai Singh: Any theories on who X could be?

Kuldeep Yadav: Of course. Of what use would I be to you without my theories?

Ajai Singh (trying to sound hurt): Don't say that, Professor saab.

Kuldeep Yadav (teasingly): Why? Can't stomach the bitter truth, Inspector saab?

Ajai Singh: Do I have to spell out what high regard I hold you in?

Kuldeep Yadav: You may have learnt many things, Singh, but not how to take a joke.

Ajai Singh: Oh.

Kuldeep Yadav: Let's return to the topic. We were talking about X?

Hari Dixit: Ji.

Kuldeep Yadav: Let's start with the obvious first. A blackmailer is murdered. A woman he was blackmailing is missing. She expressed a desire to do something drastic to her closest friend just before going missing, a day before the murder. Those are prima facie reasons to suspect Leena Puri.

Ajai Singh: But that does not square off with many other things.

Kuldeep Yadav: You told me. Nevertheless, for argument's sake, let's assume Leena Puri is X. What would that mean? How, under what conditions would that be possible?

Ajai Singh: Tell.

Kuldeep Yadav: Two conditions, basically. One: She had money, family and home that she kept secret from Bindia Sehgal – and was being blackmailed by Varun Dixit before she reconnected with Bindia Sehgal. That would explain many things. Her vulnerability to blackmail, disappearances, existence of a phone dedicated to conversations with Varun Dixit and Bindia Sehgal, frequent phone switch-offs, the fact that the first call between Leena Puri and Varun Dixit originated from Leena Puri's phone, where she hid between her two visits to Pride Apartments, where she is now.

Hari Dixit: Also why Bindia Sehgal was the only one to report her missing.

Kuldeep Yadav: Correct.

Ajai Singh: It would also mean Leena Puri may still be around Delhi-NCR? Where else would she have met Varun Dixit?

Kuldeep Yadav: Correct again.

Ajai Singh: Next point? You mentioned two conditions.

Kuldeep Yadav: She made some mistakes. First, she forgot the CD. Then, she forgot her phone. Then, returned to Pride

Apartments a week later, joined the cult meeting for some unfathomable reason and – Mistake # 3 – offered details in the meeting register that would be traceable to her.

Hari Dixit: Leena Puri seems far from innocent if those two conditions hold.

Ajai Singh: The first point I can accept. The second I don't buy.

Kuldeep Yadav: The point about mistakes?

Ajai Singh: Yes.

Kuldeep Yadav: Why? People make mistakes. Everyone does. I do, you do, Dixitji would have.

Ajai Singh: Okay, fine. Even if I take both points, the second only because you insist, one question still remains.

Kuldeep Yadav: Go on.

Ajai Singh: If the plan was to kill Varun Dixit in his apartment and the way to enter was clear, why go through the trouble of creating a parallel life? Leena Puri could as easily have gone about the same thing without introducing herself in Bindia Sehgal's life.

Hari Dixit: She might have needed monetary help at some point. Or an accomplice.

Ajai Singh: Help?

Hari Dixit: Maybe the family started suspecting something, started wondering about the money outflow. She turned to her friend for money, made up a sob story.

Ajai Singh: What about the accomplice angle?

Hari Dixit: Bindia Sehgal would have been a safer accomplice than a hired hand. Two pairs of eyes better than one to search the apartment. Someone to help hide and, later, destroy computer and phone.

Ajai Singh: You think childhood friendship is enough reason to become involved in murder?

Kuldeep Yadav (interrupting the side conversation): They were not accomplices. If they were accomplices, Bindia Sehgal wouldn't have made the missing person's complaint and she would have collected the CD from Leena Puri's apartment after her disappearance. Why do things that push the needle of suspicion towards Leena Puri?

Hari Dixit (after some thought): I agree with Professor saab here. I would also think that Leena Puri would not have had to disappear if they were accomplices. Bindia Sehgal could simply have given her an alibi if matters came to that.

Kuldeep Yadav: Absolutely.

Ajai Singh: Looks like the booze is dulling me. So what is the net of what you people are saying about Leena Puri?

Kuldeep Yadav: The net is that Leena Puri is not the killer. The narrative of Leena Puri as X is full of holes. For it to hold, we will have to agree that she went through the headache of creating a parallel life when it was not necessary and went on to make several, suicidal I would call them, mistakes.

Ajai Singh: And we aren't agreeing on any of that. Right, Dixitji?

Hari Dixit nods at Ajai Singh.

Ajai Singh: Who is X then?

Kuldeep Yadav: Let X remain X. Tell me, has it occurred to you that someone might be framing Leena Puri? I mean if Leena Puri isn't the killer, but all evidence is pointing to her…

Ajai Singh: I am not so high that I can't understand what you are saying, but I am high enough to not be thinking.

Kuldeep Yadav (makes a face): Dixitji?

Hari Dixit: Her details were entered a week later at the meeting. Why would someone do that?

Kuldeep Yadav: Why?

Hari Dixit: Oh, you asking me.

Kuldeep Yadav nods.

Hari Dixit: To show she knew how to enter the complex unnoticed.

Kuldeep Yadav: Since we have ruled out Leena Puri being X, what do you think was the intention behind revealing how Leena Puri could have entered the complex unnoticed?

Hari Dixit: To show she entered the complex unnoticed the earlier Wednesday, the day of the murder.

Kuldeep Yadav: The intention then would be to...?

Hari Dixit: ...direct suspicion towards Leena Puri.

Kuldeep Yadav: And why are we attaching importance to her entry? Why are we looking for her in connection with Varun Dixit's murder in the first place?

Hari Dixit: She was spotted with him the previous night.

Kuldeep Yadav: And? Singh, I hope you are not dozing.

Ajai Singh (with forced alertness): No, sir.

Kuldeep Yadav: Then tell me why else are we looking for Leena Puri in connection with the murder?

Hari Dixit: There was a CD with a video featuring her that Varun probably shot.

Kuldeep Yadav: A CD that was in her possession before the murder. A CD that was readily found in her apartment.

Hari Dixit: Ji.

Ajai Singh (in clearly an a-ha moment): So...if we don't treat the convenient discovery of the CD and the entry of Leena Puri's details as mistakes or forgetful behavior but a deliberate act...

Kuldeep Yadav: Woken up, Singh? Yes?

Ajai Singh: Someone is framing Leena Puri. The question is who?

Kuldeep Yadav: Simple, isn't it?

Ajai Singh: Not to me. Can't say about Dixitji.

Kuldeep Yadav: Not to you because you are drunk.

Hari Dixit: Bindia Sehgal. She was the only one who could plant the CD.

Ajai Singh: Being the only other person with keys to Leena Puri's apartment.

Kuldeep Yadav: Exactly. Awake after all, huh, Singh?

Ajai Singh: I still don't know what to make of the misplaced phone angle.

Kuldeep Yadav: Honestly, I expected a more fundamental question.

Ajai Singh looks bewildered.

Kuleep Yadav: Regarding motive.

Ajai Singh: Fine. Talk about motive.

Kuldeep Yadav: Blackmail.

Ajai Singh: Blackmail of... Bindia Sehgal? You're losing me again, Professor saab.

Kuldeep Yadav: Forget it. Let me present a theory. But before that I have a few questions for you gentlemen. Between the two of you, you would have – what? – about fifty years of police work?

Hari Dixit (looks towards Ajai Singh before replying): More or less.

Kuldeep Yadav: And how many times in those fifty years have you seen a murder frame-up orchestrated by someone else other than the killer?

Ajai Singh: Never. You, Dixitji?

Hari Dixit: Only once.

Kuldeep Yadav: Now that – and I think we are in agreement on this – Bindia Sehgal has emerged a suspect, a second question. Don't you think the entire chain of events has worked out rather...umm...conveniently for her. I mean isn't it peculiar – call it too much of a coincidence if you want – that her friend emerged suddenly from oblivion, tracked her down, took shelter in her spare apartment, disappeared soon after the murder and is now the victim of a frame-up?

Ajai Singh: It is peculiar but only cements the point about framing.

Kuldeep Yadav: It also feeds into my theory. Let me say what I have to. Ask questions afterwards.

Ajai Singh: Okay.

Kuldeep Yadav: It wasn't Leena Puri but Bindia Sehgal who was in a relationship with Varun Dixit. He started blackmailing her. She couldn't take it, decided to kill him. She knew how to enter Pride Apartments unnoticed, had possibly been there on a Wednesday during times when they were close. To frame someone else, she made up a story about a long-lost friend recently returned from America, made her appear a blackmail victim and reported her disappearance to the police a few days after the murder. Think this explains all the ends you can't close?

Ajai Singh: At least, it's woken me up.

Kuldeep Yadav: Start thinking then.

Ajai Singh: Bindia Sehgal is a...suitable...blackmail victim, for one.

Hari Dixit: What you are saying will also explain how the CD reached Pride Apartments before the murder, even before the meeting at Spiff, and how accurate details about Leena Puri came to be found in the meeting register.

Kuldeep Yadav nods.

Hari Dixit (after some thought): You are also hinting at several other things here, Professor saab. One: Bindia Sehgal arranged a second phone connection to keep in touch with Varun and that car showroom manager.

Ajai Singh: One can imagine a married woman doing that. It also solves the puzzle about how a supposed recluse like Leena Puri met Varun.

Hari Dixit: The other thing you are saying, Professor saab, is that she hatched her plan around September 2014 and started making calls to herself from the second phone to establish the existence of Leena Puri.

Ajai Singh: That complicates things. Because unknown to, but nevertheless luckily, for Bindia Sehgal, Elite Estates and Platinum Heights aren't too far off and, CDRs, if I remember correctly, said that calls between them share the same tower. Makes it difficult to establish that both phones were always with the same person.

Hari Dixit: The big question remains though. Where is Leena Puri?

Kuldeep Yadav (unable to resist a suspenseful pause): There's never been any Leena Puri.

Ajai Singh: Meaning?

Kuldeep Yadav: Remember what you told me about Platinum Heights? No maid, no Internet, no newspapers, no TV. Barely lived in. Toiletries, fridge items barely opened. As if it was a house readied for someone who did not turn up.

Hari Dixit (even as Ajai Singh processes what's been said): Those things struck us too. Also that Leena Puri, despite being short of money, always chose to arrange her own transport rather than take lifts from Bindia Sehgal who wasn't too far away.

Kuldeep Yadav (nods): While looking outside her marriage, Bindia Sehgal used the name of a childhood friend. She chatted with that showroom manager saying she was Leena Puri, right? She did the same with Varun Dixit. The laptop and phone of Varun Dixit and the phone meant for extra-marital liaisons were removed because they carried evidence of Bindia Sehgal's blackmail.

Ajai Singh: But who was the woman the neighbors saw, the woman in the CD, the woman who met Varun at Spiff?

Kuldeep Yadav: A woman whose picture Bindia Sehgal gave you claiming it was Leena Puri.

Ajai Singh (frowning): Meaning?

Kuldeep Yadav: Meaning Bindia Sehgal found someone to be seen by the neighbors and with Varun at one of his regular watering holes. And passed on the picture of that person to you. You'll remember people other than Bindia Sehgal have seen the so-called Leena Puri only twice.

Ajai Singh: And that someone agreed to appear in a video, dance and meet Varun Dixit at Bindia Sehgal's command? I don't buy it.

Kuldeep Yadav (a little angry): You should.

Ajai Singh (challenging tone): Because you are saying it? What woman would agree to be at Bindia Sehgal's beck-and-call for a thing like this?

Kuldeep Yadav (ignoring Ajai Singh): What sort of woman, Dixitji?

Hari Dixit (after some thinking, hesitantly): A…a whore?

Kuldeep Yadav (eyes twinkling): Who else?

Ajai Singh (toning down but not entirely): There's something else. You are suspecting Bindia Sehgal because the gaps in Leena Puri-as-killer theory are filled when we take Bindia Sehgal as suspect? Crime solving, I think you've forgotten today, Professor saab, isn't about making up stories.

Kuldeep Yadav: Finally, a sensible question.

Ajai Singh (mildly combative): And what do you have to say to that?

Kuldeep Yadav: There are many things you can do to test if my theory has weight.

Ajai Singh: Like?

Kuldeep Yadav:

1: Check the switch-off periods of Leena Puri's phone. They'll coincide with periods when Ashok Sehgal was in town. You said he's normally back on weekends? You'll not find a weekend when Leena Puri's phone wasn't switched off.

2: Check Leena Puri's clothes at Platinum Heights. You will find them large for a woman of her height and weight, closer to Bindia Sehgal's size. That's because Bindia Sehgal dumped her old outfits at Platinum Heights to give it a lived-in feel. Also the reason why you didn't see any of the clothes the woman hired to play Leena Puri wore. In your place, I would also check Bindia Sehgal's pictures on Facebook or whatever other social media. You may find her wearing some of the clothes you see in Platinum Heights.

3: Check electricity bills for Leena Puri's apartment from September 2014 onwards. Zero readings are all you'll find. Nobody's lived there.

4: Leena Puri recharged her prepaid connection in cash from different locations every time, right? If you get hold of Bindia Sehgal's CDRs, you will find Bindia Sehgal being around those locations on those times. Not only that, you will find Bindia

Sehgal's phone near Leena Puri's every single time. Even if you exclude calls between them from their respective residences because, as you say, they share the same tower.

5: Talk to Ratan Lal. I'll be surprised if he doesn't know Elite Estates and did not apply for a job there sometime in December 2013.

6: Check Bindia Sehgal's whereabouts on the afternoon of 17th December. My name isn't Kuldeep Yadav if there aren't gaps there. Her CDR will tell you she was around Pride Apartments on the date. When checking Bindia Sehgal's alibi, remember to show her picture to the cult people, speak to her driver. People think drivers are like walls. Without ears. They aren't.

Ajai Singh (looking at Hari Dixit): The task's cut out.

Kuldeep Yadav: If you are inclined to labor, there are two other things you could do.

Ajai Singh: What?

Kuldeep Yadav: Check Platinum Heights for fingerprints. You'll find more fingerprints of Bindia Sehgal than any other person, not what you would expect if someone else was residing there for months.

Hari Dixit: What else?.

Kuldeep Yadav (turning to Ajai Singh): If there's such a thing as a handwriting expert available to the Gurgaon police, he'll tell you the handwriting in the meeting register matches Bindia Sehgal's.

Ajai Singh: Wouldn't the easiest way to solve this be to find the woman who played Leena Puri?

Kuldeep Yadav: You can try. I have a feeling it's going to be tough. The things I mentioned are easier, quicker done. Of course, not everything will prove what I'm saying. For example the clothes could be explained as handed down, but taken together...

Hari Dixit nods.

Ajai Singh: It's almost 2 a.m.

Kuldeep Yadav: I have early morning classes tomorrow.

Ajai Singh: I told my madam I would be late. Sessions with Professor saab are always like this. She knows.

Kuldeep Yadav (addressing Dixit at first, Singh next): My reputation with his family, you can see, is in tatters. Hope you aren't using me as an excuse for other things, Singh.

Ajai Singh: Oh no, sir. *Marna hai kya maine?*

Kuldeep Yadav (addressing Dixit): I hope this wasn't a waste of your time.

Hari Dixit: Professor saab, what if we don't find things to establish the story. I mean what if...

Kuldeep Yadav (smiles): Then we can say Leena Puri exists and is the one who's framing Bindia Sehgal.

Ajai Singh: After all this mind-fucking – sorry, Dixitji, for the language – you seriously want us to look at that possibility too? You actually think that's possible?

Kuldeep Yadav: In theory, yes. Like everything is. Actually, no. Why don't we start looking at Bindia Sehgal first rather than jump to hypothetical questions?

Ajai Singh (looking towards Hari Dixit): Okay?

Hari Dixit (nods at Ajai Singh, then addresses Kuldeep Yadav): Professor saab, I wish we had met earlier.

Kuldeep Yadav: Better late than never, sir. What say, Singh?

Ajai Singh: True, true.

Kuldeep Yadav (addressing Dixit): Not for a second, Dixitji, should you allow my tone to suggest that I take death lightly. A murder is the worst crime. For murderers do what only the man upstairs should. That's unforgivable.

Ajai Singh: If there's nothing else, Dixitji, shall we leave? We will be seeing Professor saab again if needed.

Kuldeep Yadav: Always welcome, Singh. At my age, the company of good people and a little exercise for the brain can only be good.

[The gathering breaks. Ajai Singh struggles to stand erect, Hari Dixit offers a steadying hand. The Professor smiles at the sight, closes his eyes. Ajai Singh stops Hari Dixit from switching off the bulb. The visitors shuffle out.]

ಬ

Bindia Sehgal's CDR was requisitioned first thing in the morning. Inspector Bakshi agreed to move on it quickly.

ಬ

Ratan Lal confirmed applying for a job at Elite Estates in the winter of 2013. Yes, he had submitted ID papers for verification purposes. Things hadn't worked out. The family said their old driver had returned. No, he hadn't tried any other Elite Estates family before or after that. No, they weren't Sehgals but Sinhas, fellow Bihari Kayasths from neighboring Bhagalpur district.

ಬ

Hari Dixit slept on the overnight bus for the first time.

SUN JANUARY 11 2015

He saw the questions in her eyes, refused to be baited. When finally she asked in her usual gentle way *(What is happening on the case?)*, Hariji offered the reply he had rehearsed. Seems a case of personal vendetta. Varun owed someone money, was unable to pay, the person didn't take it well. Her surprise at someone killing for money, innocent woman that she was, didn't translate into a question.

Have they found the person?

Not yet, but we're close. A matter of days if our hunches are right.

It was the easiest way to say he would be leaving her again, soon. She didn't seem to mind and that, as before, was a relief. Her patience and equilibrium, he recognized, fed his resolve. Her pain was no lesser, possibly more, than his. As was her love.

Hariji went to the bathroom to hide his tears. Sarlaji teared knowing why he had left.

৪০

Something, Ashok sensed, was bothering Bindia. She missed easy chances on Scrabble, showed faint enthusiasm at evening plans, and maintained a forced smile when they met Priya and Saddie for dinner.

Jaan, something bothering you?
No, nothing.
Jaan, all fine? You seem distracted.
No, Baba. Everything's all right.
Jaan, anything on your mind? Tell me. Get it off your chest.
No, nothing. Why do you keep asking?
Late Sunday morning, Bindia felt ready, felt Ashok was ready. The opportunity was created with a distracted look when Ashok said he was leaving for the gym. He took the bait. (*Indi, tell me. I can see something's hassling you. Tell me. Get it out. Be done with it.*) She said what she had to.

There's something I've been wanting to say. [Good to see you worried, Ashok.]

Remember, my friend Leena from school. [No, you won't but this is how it's meant to go.]

She turned up a few months ago in pretty bad shape. No money, no job, generally troubled. [So far, so good.]

I...I...let her stay at Platinum, gave her some money. [Ask me how much.]

About fifty-sixty thousand. [How predictable, Ashok.]

It's meant to be a loan. [Relieved?]

I didn't tell you because I thought you wouldn't approve. I'm sorry, really sorry. [You love it when I seek approval, bow down, don't you? So, here. Go ahead. Feel thrilled. Take the chance to be Giant Heart.]

Thanks. That's not all though. [You see it doesn't end here.]

Leena went missing a month ago. The cops went to Platinum and...[Come on. Can't you see the tears welling, Ashok? Yeah. Some more handholding, it's-okaying please.]

Now the cops say she's linked to a murder, planned her disappearance. [There!]

They aren't saying it openly. Only hinting. [Balls crawling into tummy?]

I'm sorry for all this. [You want to bring in Amrit Jain this instant, don't you?]

No, no. I don't think it's necessary at this point. [The last thing I need is a lawyer asking questions.]

We've done nothing wrong. If Leena's done something, she'll have to face the cops. I just wanted you to know, not be surprised if cops drop by some day for follow-up. That's all.

Are we okay? [Of course, we are.]

Sure? [Made your day, haven't I, with all the begging?]

You're a darling, Ashok. [Could you get any more predictable?]

ॐ

The station clerk repeated the Inspector's instructions to the computer operator.

- Go to the Alumna Association website of Holy Cross Convent, Model Town. Print five copies of Bindia Sehgal's picture. Confirm if her mobile number's there.
- Use Bindia Sehgal's picture to find her on Facebook. Print her pictures in any distinctive clothing. Forget pictures in jeans, T-shirts, anything common.
- Call Inspector saab on his mobile if there's any confusion.

Before leaving for the day, the operator handed five copies of Bindia Sehgal's picture from the Alumna Association website, six separate pictures of Bindia Sehgal from Facebook, confirmed Bindia Sehgal's correct mobile number was available on the Alumna Association website.

MON JANUARY 12 2015

The man who collected the keys from Bindia Sehgal, a thicker, balder version of his Inspector saab, dropped in afterwards at the Elite Estates Resident Association (ERA) office.

Was Mrs Bindia Sehgal involved with ERA in any capacity?
Yes.
What?
She's on the Management Committee.
For how long?
Two-three years now.
In her position, would she have access to staff verification applications from residents?
Yes.
Does ERA maintain a list of all staff verification applications received?
No. We do reference checks. If those are okay, we send the papers to the police. Our role ends there.
What about cases where references aren't okay?
We inform the concerned resident.
In writing?
Over intercom.
What do you do with the rejected applications?
We dispose them.
How?

Throw them away.
Would it be possible to speak to the Sinhas?
Which one? There were two in the complex.
Both?
Sure.

Sinha # 1: No, we didn't submit any verification application for a driver in December 2013, haven't needed to in a while. Our man's good, been around for years.

Sinha # 2: Yes, we did submit an application around that time. We were told his references didn't check out. We found someone else. Sorry, I don't know who called from ERA. Our maid took the message. She's no longer with us. No idea. Her mobile doesn't work anymore. We tried a few weeks ago when we needed a full-timer again. Asked her maid-friends in the complex too. None knew. Sorry, I can't recall the driver's name. Yes, I remember he was from Bihar, from somewhere near my husband's native place actually. It may have been Ratan Lal, not sure though.

ॐ

The cult manager and his wife couldn't confirm seeing the woman in the picture. They were handed a copy to show members on Wednesday.

ॐ

The electricity meter readings for C-709, Platinum Heights were zero for September and December, near zero for October [when stuff was placed to create a life for Leena Puri?] and November [when the whore was called for an afternoon?].

Inside C-709, items of clothing were invariably large [Bindia Sehgal's] size, including two dresses similar to those worn by Bindia Sehgal in Facebook pictures. One had peacock prints. The other was in multiple shades of watermelon color.

ॐ

Inspector Bakshi called. Yes, Leena Puri's phone was generally switched off on weekends. They would have Bindia Sehgal's CDRs tomorrow morning, specific answers to their questions by evening. You assholes need to be better planned than this.

ॐ

Ajai Singh and Hari Dixit spoke around 6 p.m., agreed on several things:

- Professor Yadav had led them in the right direction.
- Abuse of Ratan Lal's ID papers couldn't conclusively be pinned on Bindia Sehgal.
- Bindia Sehgal could claim she passed on old clothes to Leena Puri.
- Bindia Sehgal could argue she wasn't the right person to answer for Leena Puri's electricity consumption patterns or phone switch-off periods.
- Evidence of Bindia Sehgal's blackmail was unlikely to be found.
- A handwriting expert could, at best, establish Bindia Sehgal's presence in Pride Apartments a week after the murder, not on the date of the murder.
- The CDRs were their best bet.
- Perhaps it was time for Hari Dixit to return.

TUE 13 JANUARY 2015

Bindia Sehgal's CDR disappointed.

Calls to and from Leena Puri were mostly traced to the same tower location, the one shared from their residences. [Nothing there. As expected.]

Since activation, Leena Puri's pre-paid connection had been recharged five times from different locations. Bindia Sehgal's phone had been used within twenty-thirty minutes of recharge time twice. On both, she seemed to have been moving from the recharge location towards her residence. [But Bindia Sehgal could claim coincidence.]

[Most disappointing] There was nothing to suggest Bindia Sehgal had been in or around Pride Apartments on the afternoon of 17th December. Her most likely location the entire afternoon? The Palladium Mall.

౮౨

Ajai Singh: Hello, hello. Sir?

Kuldeep Yadav: Yes, Singh.

Ajai Singh: Can we talk now?

Kuldeep Yadav: Is it very urgent? I'm between classes.

Ajai Singh: Five minutes only. Something about the Dixit case.

Kuldeep Yadav: Okay.

Ajai Singh: Things are like you said. Leena Puri's flat has zero electricity consumption. Clothes inside are Bindia Sehgal's size. At least two dresses match what Bindia Sehgal is seen wearing in Facebook posts. We also know she had access to Ratan Lal's ID papers.

Kuldeep Yadav: What about phone switch-off periods?

Ajai Singh: Switched off when Ashok Sehgal was in town.

Kuldeep Yadav: What's the problem then?

Ajai Singh: CDRs don't show Bindia Sehgal around Pride Apartments on the day of the murder.

Kuldeep Yadav: Did the cult people recognize her picture?

Ajai Singh: The manager and his wife aren't sure. We left a picture to check with other members. We will know tomorrow.

Kuldeep Yadav: Hmm.

Ajai Singh: Even if someone recognizes, all it will confirm is Bindia Sehgal's presence in Pride Apartments...

Kuldeep Yadav: ...a week after the murder.

Ajai Singh: Yes.

Kuldeep Yadav: That isn't enough for you?

Ajai Singh: Chances of evidence of Bindia Sehgal's blackmail being found are nil. To take her in, we need to establish her presence in Pride Apartments on the afternoon of the murder.

Kuldeep Yadav: Her phone was at the mall all afternoon?

Ajai Singh: Tower information is for a radius around the area. She once said she was at the mall that afternoon. That's why we're saying.

Kuldeep Yadav: Look, one thing's clear. We aren't wrong about Bindia Sehgal.

Ajai Singh: Not after what we've found in the last few days.

Kuldeep Yadav: If it's clear we aren't wrong about her and if it's clear her phone was at the mall, it follows she got out of the mall and went to Pride Apartments.

Ajai Singh: Okay.

Kuldeep Yadav: My suggestion? Seek her alibi. She'll say she was at the mall all along. That can't – simply can't – be true. She left the mall, almost certainly without her driver. Speak to taxi stands, do whatever else you policemen do. Ask questions, repeat, crosscheck. I don't need to tell you there will be a hole somewhere.

Ajai Singh: What about the phone being in the mall? That's what's bothering us most.

Kuldeep Yadav: Singh, what's with you? Think.

Ajai Singh: She forgot it behind?

Kuldeep Yadav: From what you have learnt about her, do you think that's likely?

Ajai Singh (softly): No.

Kuldeep Yadav: Then?

Ajai Singh: She left it behind deliberately, in anticipation of exactly this kind of situation?

Kuldeep Yadav: No. She doesn't know mobile phone location is traceable even when it isn't in use. Otherwise, we wouldn't have Leena Puri's phone, basically the second phone, switched off in Gurgaon.

Ajai Singh: Then?

Kuldeep Yadav: I don't have time. Else I would have extracted the answer from your mouth.

Ajai Singh: Say it, sirji. Go back to your students.

Kuldeep Yadav: Tell me, why do some of your *sarkari* brethren discourage people with mobile phones in their offices?

Ajai Singh: They worry bribe demands or exchanges will be recorded.

Kuldeep Yadav: So?

Ajai Singh (pleased with himself): So...Varun Dixit barred Bindia Sehgal from carrying her phone when they met. He worried she might record their conversation, come to us.

Kuldeep Yadav: Well done. I won't be surprised if her driver says she tends to forget the phone in the car sometimes.

Ajai Singh: We could have done this quicker.

Kuldeep Yadav: Meaning I should have done your job for you?

Ajai Singh: I'm hanging up.

Kuldeep Yadav: One more thing.

Ajai Singh: What?

Kuldeep Yadav: Now that you have the CDRs, check Bindia Sehgal's calls about a week before each of the two sightings of the so-called Leena Puri. If there are any common numbers that have never been called before or since, find whom they belong to. They could lead you to the whore or her pimp.

Ajai Singh: I thought you didn't want us spending time looking for the whore.

Kuldeep Yadav: I did, Singh. But we are dealing with someone very clever here. Don't be surprised if her alibi is solid. If it is, only that woman can help us.

Ajai Singh: For your information, whores and pimps are into WhatsApp and that other thing...Snapdeal...Snapchat... something like that...these days. I don't know how useful the CDRs will prove.

Kuldeep Yadav: I don't know either. But what else do you want to do? Let a killer get away?

WED JANUARY
14 2015

No cult member could say with certainty if they had seen the woman in the picture on the 24th. Earlier in the day, a grumpy Inspector Bakshi reported no phone number sticking out in Bindia Sehgal's CDR for the 13th to 20th November 2014 and 9th to 16th December 2014 periods.

Dixitji, it's all down to the alibi now.

༄

Bindia Sehgal had no follow up question after his response to why there was sudden interest in her whereabouts. His response had been stock-evasive: Leenaji's disappearance, you are aware, has been linked to the Dixit case. In asking your whereabouts, we are only trying to cover all angles. It's routine.

She couldn't recall her whereabouts on the afternoon of 24th December. The 17th she remembered. Returning home from The Palladium, they had been stuck in a massive traffic jam near HUDA City Center Metro Station.

༄

Except the trip to The Palladium on the 17th, Pancham remembered nothing special about either Wednesday.

He usually drove madam around. There were times when she took the car alone, but he knew of those because she collected the keys from him.

He picked the keys to the two cars every morning at 8.30 a.m., cleaned them, held both keys till the end of duty hours at 7 p.m.

True, he wouldn't know if she stepped out alone after his duty hours.

The Palladium was a regular haunt for madam. So much so, he knew locations of all nine gates. Madam's visit there could be anywhere between two to five hours. He normally dropped her at Gate # 1, parked in the basement, picked her from whichever gate she asked.

No, he hadn't heard of a Leena madam, not noticed anything different in Bindia madam's behavior or routine in recent times, not driven her to any new location in recent times, not worked overtime in a while.

Yes, there were days she did not step out of the house at all.

Yes, there were times she forgot the mobile phone in the car. Not sure if that happened on the 17th though.

What do I say? The shopping bags are always heavy. I would remember only if they were light on some day.

ॐ

Late evening, they made a timeline for the afternoon.

The Afternoon Of 17 December 2014		
According To Bindia Sehgal (And Pancham Chauhan)		
Time	Likely Happening	Remarks
About 1.30 p.m.	Bindia Sehgal left home for The Palladium with driver Pancham Chauhan	As per Bindia Sehgal; confirmed by Pancham Chauhan
1.45-1.50 p.m.	Bindia Sehgal reached The Palladium	
2.01 p.m.	Bindia Sehgal purchased a tie for her husband using a credit card	Transaction confirmation on Bindia Sehgal's phone (Amount: Rs. 1,125; Place: The Tie Company)
2.26 p.m.	Bindia Sehgal purchased some home décor stuff using a credit card	Transaction confirmation on Bindia Sehgal's phone (Amount: Rs. 6,893; Place: HSH)
5.03 p.m.	Bindia Sehgal paid at a spa using a credit card	Transaction confirmation on Bindia Sehgal's phone (Amount: Rs. 7,300; Place: Malini's)
About 5.15 p.m.	Bindia Sehgal left The Palladium for home with driver Pancham Chauhan	As per Bindia Sehgal; confirmed by Pancham Chauhan
6.30 p.m.	Bindia Sehgal reached home	
Note: The possibility of the phone being left behind in the car is acknowledged by both, but confirmed by neither.		

The time gap between the second and third credit card transaction prompted them to a draw up a second timeline.

The Afternoon Of 17 December 2014		
According To Ajai Singh (And Hari Dixit)		
Time	Likely Happening	Remarks
About 1.30 p.m.	Bindia Sehgal left home for The Palladium with driver Pancham Chauhan	As per Bindia Sehgal; confirmed by Pancham Chauhan
1.45- 1.50 p.m.	Bindia Sehgal reached The Palladium	
2.01 p.m.	Bindia Sehgal purchased a tie for her husband using a credit card	Transaction confirmation on Bindia Sehgal's phone (Amount: Rs. 1,125; Place: The Tie Company)
2.26 p.m.	Bindia Sehgal purchased some home décor stuff using a credit card	Transaction confirmation on Bindia Sehgal's phone (Amount: Rs. 6,893; Place: HSH)
About 2.30 p.m.	Bindia Sehgal left The Palladium for Pride Apartments in a taxi	Bindia Sehgal engaged a half-day taxi. Finding another one for return from near Pride Apartments wasn't easy.
About 2.45 p.m.	Bindia Sehgal entered the Pride Apartments complex (Cult members would have been arriving for their 3 p.m. meeting)	On an afternoon, it wouldn't have taken more than 15 minutes from The Palladium
About 3 p.m.	Bindia Sehgal served sedative-laced tea to Varun Dixit	
About 3.20 p.m.	Varun Dixit was stabbed	Sedatives took 15-20 minutes to act

The Afternoon Of 17 December 2014		
According To Ajai Singh (And Hari Dixit)		
Time	Likely Happening	Remarks
3.24 p.m.	Varun Dixit's phone was switched off	Varun Dixit's CDR
About 4.30 p.m.	Bindia Sehgal left for The Palladium after cleaning up	
About 4.45 p.m.	Bindia Sehgal returned to The Palladium	
5.19 p.m.	Bindia Sehgal paid at a spa using a credit card	Transaction confirmation on Bindia Sehgal's phone (Amount: Rs. 7,300; Place: Malini's)
About 5.30 p.m.	Bindia Sehgal left The Palladium for home with driver Pancham Chauhan	As per Bindia Sehgal; confirmed by Pancham Chauhan
About 6/ 6.30 p.m.	Bindia Sehgal reached home	

৪৩

[Scene: SHO Ajai Singh's Office, Vikrant Vihar Police Station.]

[The Inspector and Hari Dixit look tired, are in conversation.]

Ajai Singh: There are two things we need to do tomorrow at the mall, Dixitji. First, check how long she was inside the spa. Second, show her picture at the taxi stand.

Hari Dixit: What if the spa people say she was inside longer than we thought? The bill amount doesn't suggest a short stop.

Ajai Singh looks distracted, rubs eyes vigorously.

Hari Dixit: What if the driver she used that afternoon isn't there at the stand? Or, what if he's there and doesn't remember?

Ajai Singh (continues rubbing eyes): Then we will have to go to our new friend.

Hari Dixit (confused): Who?

Ajai Singh (half-smiles): Hopefully, the CCTV footage will tell us she left the mall at 2.30 p.m., returned at 5 p.m. Maybe we'll get a taxi number too.

Hari Dixit: That'll take time.

Ajai Singh: To be honest, it may not be sufficient either. Her absence from the mall between 2.30 and 5 p.m. does not automatically place her at Pride Apartments.

Hari Dixit (sensing the fatigue in Ajai Singh's voice): We'll get to know tomorrow.

Ajai Singh (starts wrapping up): Yes, tomorrow. 11 a.m.? Nothing opens before that.

Hari Dixit: Ji. 11 a.m.

৪৩

More questions occurred to them in their respective beds.

Some pertinent:

- How had Bindia Sehgal entered The Palladium with a knife, twice?
  There was security, metal detectors. True, they relaxed when it came to a woman, but still...
- Had Bindia Sehgal disposed the knife on the way back to The Palladium?
  Unlikely. Of course, there were a few places en route one could think of where a knife could be dumped, but that

would've meant stopping the taxi when on a tight schedule, raising the driver's suspicions.

Others pointless:

- How had the laptop and phone been carried?
  In shopping bags or handbag! Mall security wouldn't be bothered about a laptop and phone anyway.
- When had they been disposed?
  Certainly not en route the mall. That would have been noticed, suspicious. Maybe the night of 17th or 18th once Pancham had left for the day. Not the 19th for that was Friday when her husband usually returned.
- How had they been disposed?
  Burning would take time, raise a stink. But in that lonely house, there was time to crush, pack the bits.
- Where had they been disposed?
  Anywhere! With husband away, Pancham gone after 7 p.m., no one else around and Elite Estates' security unlikely to record a resident's movements, she could have gone to the bloody Yamuna!

THU JANUARY
15 2015

Nobody remembered the woman in the picture at the taxi stand. There were so many passengers, so many drivers including non-regulars. A vehicle number would help.

৵

Malini's, the spa, was a darker, bigger, more fragrant version of the cult manager's home. The heavily made-up, heavy woman at the counter said they could tell how long the client had stayed only after looking at the bill. The bill couldn't be found immediately. The server was down since yesterday. The technical team was on it, hoped to get it running in the next hour or so. Could they come a little later?

৵

Mall security cooperated, run latest facial recognition software using Bindia Sehgal's photograph on all gate footage between 1.30 and 6 p.m., said she entered via Gate # 1 at 1.47 p.m., exited via Gate # 4 at 5.32 p.m., didn't leave the mall during the period.

But she had. Where was she in the mall between 2.30 and 5.30 p.m.?

That's the interesting part, sir. We don't see her anywhere during that period.

Meaning what? She didn't leave and she wasn't around?

That's what, sir. In the window you mention, we see her at 2.27 p.m. in C-Wing, ground floor and then again at…at 5.24 p.m., D-Wing, second floor.

Not once in between? Nowhere?

No, sir.

Let me guess. C-wing, Ground Floor is where HSH is. D-wing, Second Floor…you said…is where Malini's is.

Sir.

How's that possible? She had to be somewhere.

The security manager insisted the system was glitch-free.

Sure?

Yes, sir. Absolutely.

100 percent sure? No one can get out or come in without being seen on CCTV? Understand that this is a murder case. No ordinary victim either. A policeman's son.

Uh…umm…there are a few entry-exit blind spots.

Go on.

There's a coffee shop – Tidbits – with outdoor seating where a small exit is unmonitored. Plus, someone who gets off in the basement parking and uses a service lift can come in unnoticed.

How close are HSH and Malini's to these unmonitored points?

Here's the floor plan, Sir. HSH is here. Tidbits is…one, two, three…three shops away. Malini's is here. One of the service lifts opens less than four feet away from it.

This service lift…if one were to stop at the ground floor…
…would be close to Gate # 4.
So, both nearby?
Sir.
Where's the taxi stand?
Here.
Not far if one exited from Tidbits?
In fact, the closest exit to the taxi stand is the one from Tidbits.
So, someone who used the Tidbits exit and re-entered via basement service lift wouldn't show on CCTV.
Yes. But that person would have to know the blind spots. That's not common knowledge.
Possible to see footage of basement parking entry nearest to service lift near Malini's?
Are we looking for anything specific?
Yes. Taxis that entered between 4.30 and 5 p.m. on 17th December. Passengers inside too.
Vehicle number shouldn't be a problem. Passenger images will be difficult. That's how the camera is positioned.
Registration numbers of taxis that entered during that time then. How long will it take?
Fifteen-twenty minutes.

ॐ

They had come through Gate # 1 themselves, seen the checks on women. The smarter the woman, the more perfunctory the check. Yes, it was possible to smuggle in a knife. But would she have dared to get inside with a murder weapon later, however lax the security, however cleaned-up the knife?

The answer to that question came in the basement. Within seconds of exiting the service lift that led to Malini's. There was no guard, no metal detector.

ॐ

Two taxis dropped passengers near the service lift, sir.

Numbers?

XX-XX-XXXX and XX-XX-XXXX.

Picture of driver or passenger?

Not possible, sir. I told you. Camera angles are such.

At least print us the clearest shot of the woman you have from the day. Something that shows what clothes she was wearing, bags she was carrying. The larger the print, the better.

This size?

Fine if that's the best you can do.

This one works? Or would you prefer this one?

Give both.

Picture # 1: Bindia Sehgal in blue jeans, lemon green sweater, goggles perched on head, large black bag hanging from shoulder. [Bag large enough to carry a laptop.] Peeping from the black shoulder bag: a red tie with green and yellow Santa Clauses.

Picture # 2: Bindia Sehgal in blue jeans, lemon green sweater, goggles perched on head, large black bag hanging from shoulder. In hand: a large pink HSH cloth bag. Peeping from the pink bag: the same tie.

Before we go, one last question.

Sir.

Think carefully before you reply. I want a Yes or No answer only.

Sir.

Suppose someone doesn't know about your cameras, wants to get out and return quickly unnoticed using a taxi. Imagine it's a matter of life and death for them.

Okay.

Imagine being registered present at Malini's is important for them for some reason. Imagine they are carrying a knife with them on their way back.

Okay.

Will they exit from Tidbits because it's closest to the taxi stand?

Yes, sir.

Will they enter via the basement and use the service lift because there will be no security or metal detectors?

Yes, sir.

Think again. Would you say that's the route one would take if one were pressed for time, needed to bring in a knife, wanted to be seen at Malini's last?

Yes, sir. Even if they were not aware of the cameras, they would still do that.

Then the fact they are not seen on CCTV can be explained? Not because the person knew the blind spots, but because it was the most practical thing to do in their circumstances.

Yes, sir. Then we can say they did what was the most... practical...thing and it's only a matter of luck that they escaped the CCTV.

Okay. And stop calling your security foolproof.

ॐ

Yes, the system's up.

A customer of yours paid Rs 7,300 via credit card at 5.19 p.m. on 17th December. We want to know how long she was here.

She opted for two services. A Balinese massage for Rs 7,000. Eyebrow for Rs 300.

How long do those take?

Eyebrow is a fifteen minute job. The massage is between one-and-a-half to two hours.

The credit card transaction was at 5.19 p.m. You're saying the customer would have come here at 3 p.m.?

Roughly.

Pucca?

Yes. Around 3 p.m.

You would have a record of that? No, sir. We just keep billing records.

Only bills?

Appointments for massages and other long duration services too.

Can we see the appointment schedule for the person who did her massage?

Sure. Here. This is Melody's schedule for 17th December. Wait a second. There's something wrong.

What?

Melody had a bridal make-up session appointment till 4.30 p.m.

So she couldn't have done the massage?

Right. But...let me check her bills for the day.

Okay. The bridal make-up session was billed at 4.27 p.m.

Which means she either did the massage or the bridal make-up, but couldn't have done both?

Yes.

Is the girl around?

Yes.

I remember. You wouldn't, Reeta madam. Komal madam was on duty that day. This customer got only eyebrow done. Paid for the massage too. Said she had got the massage done from me earlier but found the credit card transaction reversed in a later statement. So, was repaying. We talked about her honesty after she left.

ॐ

The first driver was the right one. Yes, he remembered taking her to Pride Apartments on an afternoon. Date he couldn't be sure about, but he remembered the tie in the picture. Who in their right mind wore a tie with Santa Baba pictures?

ॐ

Dixitji, I think we now have enough to take her in, draw out a confession.

Little did they know of the twist to follow.

Part - III

Murder in the murderer is no such ruinous thought as poets and romancers will have it; it does not unsettle him, or fright him from his ordinary notice of trifles; it is an act quite easy to be contemplated.

—Ralph Waldo Emerson

Nobody's ever been arrested for a murder; they have only ever been arrested for not planning it properly.

—Terry Hayes

FRI 16 JANUARY 2015

There came a time when I started looking outside marriage. I felt lonely, unwanted. Longed, prayed, itched for love. Not the sort of love family and friends offer, but the sort that lovers – spouses, boyfriends – do. Even with lover-type love I wasn't looking for physical intimacy or love of the till-death-do-us-part and I-will-do-anything-for-you-and-vice-versa variety. Those can involve complications. I didn't want complications.

The goal, if that is the word, was a very limited kind of love. Where a lover would make me feel desired, precious, lift my mood and self-esteem. With banter and the occasional (innocent?) touch. They didn't have to be sincere either. Just acting sincere would be enough. Net: (1) I was desperate for male attention, prepared to indulge whoever threw it my way; and, (2) I was prepared to be used by men, and use men. Up to a point.

Leena said I could use her name. It'll take away the guilt, she said. She was right, always knew better.

Leena left school and country a long time ago, never to be seen or heard again. She kept her promise though, stayed in my head. I kept my promise too, never let anyone know. She was the ideal friend: available when needed, listening patiently to the smallest peeve, never judging, egging me to do things I wouldn't normally bring myself to. It was at her suggestion that I took on Dadi for her tough love, bore Ashok's initially hammy wooing, let go of Jai.

I met Varun during that crazy phase. We clicked instantly, started meeting, talking. Arranging a second mobile phone connection helped.

We first met at a party. I was desperate, vulnerable; he was kind, attentive, mildly – but unambiguously – flirty. We hit it off, met the next day. The second meeting was as good as the first and, though I nicely refused to share my mobile number, we agreed to meet again a few days later.

I did realize though that a second mobile phone connection would be needed soon. Using the primary mobile number was out of the question. There was another recent male acquaintance asking and a third had discernibly lost ardor after delay in number exchange.

ERA had received a driver verification application from the Sinhas. Complete with recent photograph, identity and address proof copies. I took those to a TelStar kiosk, got them to issue a prepaid connection. A postpaid connection would have meant bills being sent to the poor man's address or creating an e-trail. The connection, taken for a large validity time and amount to avoid frequent recharge, has been recharged from different locations since.

Mobile phone numbers were exchanged during the third meeting. The Sinhas were told the driver's references didn't check out. The message was passed on through their maid. At afternoon time, when both Sinha cars were away.

With Varun, one thing led to another.

There were long phone conversations. About life's greatest regrets. About people missed most in life. About the rank money, fame, family, friends, love and sex occupied in our respective life-priorities.

The physical contact began with awkward shoulder-first hugs. Things went up several notches on the first movie date. Pre-interval, we held hands. Post-interval, he sucked my fingers. Sex became unavoidable after a point, happened the first time after he leered in an exciting way while I browsed at Ashley & Drew's. I could have lived without the sex, but denying him would have meant losing him. And because I wasn't denying it, I decided to enjoy it.

The blackmail began in end March. He had filmed me secretly.

He called me home for the first time (*Don't bring your mobile.*), played a CD, made his demand. A one-time payment of Rs fifteen lakh or an EMI (his words) of Rs 75,000 by the fifteenth of every month. In cash. I threatened, cried, begged, foolishly offered to lure another woman. God knows I know enough randy cash cows. He wasn't listening.

The EMI option was taken. Because fifteen lakh is a lot of cash. Because there was no guarantee a one-time payment would not lead to another demand. Because EMIs offered comfort that the video wouldn't surface anytime soon. The finally agreed EMI was Rs 50,000. I sold some jewelry, started paying.

That first visit to Pride Apartments had been on a Wednesday afternoon. I noticed people enter the complex unasked, saw the notice directing first-timers to the meditation group meeting venue. The knowledge came handy later.

One day something snapped inside me.

It was Payment Day, September. We met in a basement parking lot, inside his car. I passed the five hundred rupees bundle. The location and denomination were important, for he liked to count the amount. Twice. He counted, re-counted, found the bundle two notes short, snapped his fingers angrily. As if he owned me.

I decided I had had enough, decided he had to die.

What right did he have to humiliate me like this? How long could I allow myself to be twirled around his fingers? How long could I live in fear?

Leena seconded the idea, offered to take the fall.

Her logic was simple yet unarguable: Leena Puri is the one he has fucked, the one he is blackmailing, the one who can disappear never to be found, the one who can shield you forever.

For my own sanity and good, I would have to let go of Leena though. Never bring her name to my lips, her memory to my head. *In a sense, Bindia, there will be two murders. I will kill him. You will kill me. Then there will be closure, peace. Believe me, there will be.*

I did as always.

ॐ

We planned a long time.

Some things were clear from the start:

- It would all be between the two of us. Third party involvement was risky.

    So, there would be no hired hand, no attempt to get hold of a gun. A knife would have to do.

- He had to die in his own home.
  How else would evidence of our relationship be collected?
- A Wednesday afternoon close to Payment Day in December was the best time.
  Enough time to plan, but not to reconsider!
- He, strong fellow, would have to be sedated before the knifing.
- Evidence linking Varun and Leena had to be created, left for the police to find.
  Evidence that Varun knew Leena, that he was blackmailing her, that Leena knew how to reach his place undetected, that Leena had recovered what he had held against her.
  Of course, there was no Leena outside my head. One had to be found!
  Someone who would be seen with Varun not long before his murder, someone who would be willing to feature in a slutty video, someone who would be seen by the neighbors in an apartment where the video would be found. Someone not from Delhi-NCR whose picture I could share with the police when the missing person complaint for Leena was made.
- I would have an alibi for the afternoon. Not with a person (no third party involvement!) but at a place. A place not too far from Pride Apartments with no traffic bottlenecks en route. A place where I would register presence before and after the deed. A place where I would readily find a half-day taxi to go to and return from Pride Apartments.
  The Palladium!

৪৩

Finding a home for Leena, the home where the CD with which Varun was supposedly blackmailing her would be found, was easy. Ashok and I had a flat where we had dumped some of our old furniture, utensils and a fridge. We threw in a few of my old clothes and shoes and some groceries and toileteries to give it the lived-in look.

Megha, a Mumbai-based prostitute, became Leena's face. It was her snap that accompanied the missing person's complaint for Leena, her online 'promo' video that passed as the blackmail material Varun had held.

How did I find Megha? Earlier in the year, Hema had shared four video promos. Two girls, two guys. The Notty@Forty gang was asked to pick one each as 'touch-allowed' dancers for her Twentieth Wedding Anniversary Bachelorette. Megha was the one we had rejected for looking old.

All Hema learnt was that a Delhi-based friend fancied Megha for her bachelorette. 'Really? The one we said no to. To each their own, I guess. You will need to get in touch with Sanjay, her agent. I will WhatsApp his details. Use WhatsApp with him. They prefer it that way.'

We flew Megha to Delhi twice. On both occasions, she was told she would be my 'gift' to a lover.

Sanjay wanted advance payment. Drop the cash with Avnish at the Timbuktoo boutique in Jewel Hotel. Any day except Sunday between 11 a.m. and 6 p.m. Tell Avnish you are a friend of Sanjay Nagpal, show the message specifying the amount, pay. The rest will be taken care of. Avnish was nothing like what I had imagined. For one, Avnish was a woman.

The first time I took Megha to Pride Apartments, I made her sit for a while (He should be here anytime soon.), feigned a debilitating headache, requested her to get some milk for tea from the neighbors (I will need to wait here. He can come any moment.), told her when she returned that he wouldn't be able to make it because his uncle had had a heart attack.

Megha's milk search was important. At least one neighbor in that under-occupied building would see the woman who the police believed was Leena. We learnt later she knocked two doors. Better.

On 14th December, I called Varun, requested meeting at Spiff around 9 p.m. on the 16th. There was a chance I would be able to raise cash for one-time settlement by January, wanted to discuss how matters would be closed. The December payment could be exchanged in the Spiff car park before or after the meeting. Not surprisingly, he was open to the idea.

That set the schedule for Megha's second visit, meant to make up for the boyfriend's – and my own – disappointment over the earlier cancellation. She was told to meet up with Varun at Spiff at 9 p.m. Spiff was a deliberate choice. Varun went there often. A woman recently seen in his company wouldn't go unnoticed. Which is what happened. He, of course, was expecting me.

Close to meeting hour, knowing Varun would arrive sharp at 9 p.m., I WhatsApped saying I might be delayed. Bad traffic.

While he waited, Megha reached Spiff, introduced herself to Varun as the gift from Jia (the name I had given her, Sanjay and Avnish), received a message relayed through Sanjay to leave immediately. The night's plans were cancelled. The clients had had a fight. Varun probably thought it was a case of mistaken identity.

A little after 9.30 p.m., once Sanjay confirmed Megha's exit from Spiff, I WhatsApped Varun about having been caught by cops jumping a red light. Can we meet tomorrow afternoon, your place? We can discuss final payment. Also notes this time are smaller denomination. Counting could take longer. He agreed. The phone was switched off. We didn't need it anymore.

That's how a Wednesday afternoon meeting was set in his apartment. The CD of Megha was already at Platinum Heights. There was no point risking being seen there after Varun's demise and Leena's disappearance.

On 17th December, I went to The Palladium. Getting off at Gate # 1 was deliberate. Pancham usually dropped me there. Variation from routine was best avoided. The knife was in a Kitchen Kitsch bag. Had security asked, they would have been told it was for return for a faulty handle.

I made credit card purchases to establish alibi, slipped out in the afternoon through the exit closest to the taxi stand, took a taxi to Pride Apartments, asked the taxi driver to wait.

To administer the sedative, I offered to make tea while Varun counted. (Thanks, Niti, but the pills weren't for my sleeplessness.) Once he fell, I plunged the knife with all might, switched off the mobile phone, located the CD (thankfully in the place where he had taken it out from earlier), collected the laptop, cleaned every surface touched, washed the knife.

The taxi dropped me back at the basement, near the service lift that led to Malini's. At Malini's, a third credit card transaction was made, some extra money shelled out to suggest I had been there long.

The knife, laptop and phone were not disposed the same night. The area around the HUDA City Center Metro Station had been swarming with cops and there was no point taking chances. Nevertheless the laptop and phone were pounded into pieces, packed in three separate garbage bags, thrown the next night in separate places. The knife was boiled in hot water like

TV guys said it was in the Aarushi case. It remains in my kitchen. Unused.

A second trip was made to Pride Apartments a week later. Another taxi, another mall. Leena's details were entered in the logbook the meditation group maintained.

The story was ready for the police, if/ when they came.

ॐ

Leena Puri, best friend from school, called one September morning. It was a surprise. She hadn't been seen or heard since she left school and country.

We met at a coffee shop. Leena looked terribly down, said she had returned to India recently, had no money, nowhere to go. Things clearly weren't all right with her. Uncle, she said, had passed away a few years ago. Something else she said suggested there had either been no marriage or the marriage hadn't worked. Her mother passed away when she was young. There had been no siblings.

We have an empty flat where we have dumped some old furniture and a fridge. I offered her stay there and some money. During conversations, Leena wasn't forthcoming about what was wrong. I didn't press. She was, I sensed, looking for space to sort things out in her head and I respected that. She refused to socialize, would either not take calls sometimes or shut off the phone for a day or two.

Sixteenth December, when we went shopping to Hauz Khas Village, was the last I saw her. Later the same day, she made a weird call. Had I not been busy trying to reach my son at boarding school, I would have probed. Not sure whether she would have obliged though. Had it not been Peshawar Killing Day, the plan was to say I was down with a severe migraine. An old problem for which I had medical papers if things came to that.

I tried calling her later in the night, found her phone switched off. When it stayed that way for the next two-three days, I decided to go to the police. She had switched off for a few days before, but the call preceding this particular disappearance was worrying.

Three things about the story had to be stuck to:

- Leena reached out in September.
  Evidence of calls between us could be created only September onwards. If we had reconnected earlier, the police would wonder why we hadn't spoken earlier.
  The September reach out, we realized in time, had others pluses too. When they found Leena Puri's phone registered in another name and in use for longer than what Bindia Sehgal had been told, the police would think of Leena as a liar and manipulator. A person not above murder!
- It appeared things hadn't gone well for Leena in life.
  That provided reason for offering Leena use of the Platinum Heights flat, the location most convenient to create a life for her.
- Leena was not forthcoming about her past, generally reclusive, seeking privacy.
  That would explain the phone switch-offs, contact with a limited number of people, why Bindia Sehgal didn't know of her friend's blackmail. And, importantly, Bindia could always say 'I don't know/ She never told' if the police posed a tricky question.

We chose to go the police because disappearance would cement police suspicion about Leena, lull them into thinking the murderer had been identified, send them on a hunt for someone who couldn't be found.

൭

Woman Held For Paramour-Turned-Blackmailer's Murder

By InExpress News Service | Published: 16 January 2015 11:02 a.m. | Last Updated: 16 January 2015 11:02 a.m.

Gurgaon: The police yesterday arrested Bindia Sehgal (43), a resident of posh Elite Estates, for the murder of Varun Dixit (32). Dixit was knifed to death in his own apartment on 17 December 2014. The accused is married to a high-ranking MNC executive and the couple has a fourteen-year-old son. Dixit, Sehgal's one-time paramour, was said to have been blackmailing her for several months, threatening to upload a secretly recorded video on a prominent social networking site.

Police say Sehgal has confessed and admit to being astounded by her meticulous planning. 'She not only worked out a solid alibi but went to extraordinary lengths to frame a fictional female friend,' said ACP Nishant Bhasin.

According to police sources, on the day of the murder, Sehgal shopped using a credit card at a mall near the victim's residence, proceeded to his house, committed the deed after drugging him and returned to make another credit card transaction at the same mall. Service lifts were used to smuggle the murder weapon, a knife, into the mall. The date and time for the murder was carefully chosen – a Wednesday afternoon when the victim's complex sees a stream of visitors for a meditation group meeting. The victim's laptop, phone and a CD that held the secretly recorded video were taken and destroyed later. Officials who first visited the crime scene recall the victim's apartment being wiped clear of fingerprints.

Sehgal, the police said, also tried to frame a fictional friend for Dixit's murder. She made a missing person complaint regarding an old friend soon after the murder and ensured that the person whose photograph she had shared with the police was seen with Dixit the night before his murder. A video of the same person was left for the police to conveniently find and lead them into thinking the missing friend had been blackmailed by Dixit and had disappeared after murdering him.

'The photograph and video were drawn from the online profile of a Mumbai-based dancer-cum-sex worker. The woman was flown to Delhi and paid for being seen with Dixit at one of his regular watering holes,' said Bhasin. The police believe that the Mumbai woman was misled and ruled out further investigation into her role in the Dixit murder.

৪০

Hariji called home. Sarlaji, we found the culprit. She's confessed.

It was a woman?

Yes.

—

They were in a relationship. She was married, feared being discovered. [Stop. No need to mention blackmail. If she discovers later, say: Yes, she claims Varun was blackmailing her. It's just a false claim to get some sympathy, a lighter sentence. No truth in it.]

—

Sarlaji?

You return tomorrow?

Tomorrow morning. The bus leaves in an hour. All of you are okay?

The girls have been missing you.

I've been missing them too. The work here is over.

What do you want for breakfast?

Sarlaji, don't, don't cry.

౭౩

Hari Dixit held the Inspector's hand.

Leaving, Dixitji?

Yes.

Good. Good.

I...I...don't know what to say.

You don't need to say anything.

Thank you. Without you...

You would have done the same in my place. Is it not?

—

Then?

—

Dixitji, Dixitji. Go home in peace. Your work here is over. One minute. Hello. Where? B-187? Who? Okay. We'll leave now.

Another body, Inspector saab?

I can drop you at the bus stand. It's on the way.